"I Need You, Sheila."

He massaged her shoulder, felt her shudder. "Is there some man in your life who would object to our being friends?"

"I'm not involved with anyone right now," she told him.

"Then why—"

"Because I don't have room in my life for you, Caleb Bishop!" she said, pulling out of his grasp.

Caleb jerked her up against him and brought his mouth forcefully down on hers.

She tried to fight the urge to melt into him, to give herself over to his assault, but the effort failed. She responded to his brutal kiss with equal fury.

This mad dizziness was a unique sensation. Sheila hadn't felt anything like it since the last time Caleb kissed her. The night she had given him her virginity and her heart—and he had given her Danny.

The child he didn't know he had fathered.

D0198310

Dear Reader,

Spring is in the air—and all thoughts turn toward love. With six provocative romances from Silhouette Desire, you too can enjoy a season of new beginnings…and happy endings!

Our March MAN OF THE MONTH is Lass Small's *The Best Husband in Texas*. This sexy rancher is determined to win over the beautiful widow he's loved for years! Next, Joan Elliott Pickart returns with a wonderful love story— *Just My Joe*. Watch sparks fly between handsome, wealthy Joe Dillon and the woman he loves.

Don't miss Beverly Barton's new miniseries, 3 BABIES FOR 3 BROTHERS, which begins with *His Secret Child*. The town golden boy is reunited with a former flame—and their child. Popular Anne Marie Winston offers the third title in her BUTLER COUNTY BRIDES series, as a sexy heroine forms a partnership with her lost love in *The Bride Means Business*. Then an expectant mom matches wits with a brooding rancher in Carol Grace's *Expecting....* And Virginia Dove debuts explosively with *The Bridal Promise,* when star-crossed lovers marry for convenience.

This spring, please write and tell us why you read Silhouette Desire books. As part of our 20th anniversary celebration in the year 2000, we'd like to publish some of this fan mail in the books—so drop us a line, tell us how long you've been reading Desire books and what you love about the series. And enjoy our March titles!

Regards,

Joan Marlow Golan
Senior Editor, Silhouette Desire

Please address questions and book requests to:
Silhouette Reader Service
U.S.: 3010 Walden Ave., P.O. Box 1325, Buffalo, NY 14269
Canadian: P.O. Box 609, Fort Erie, Ont. L2A 5X3

HIS SECRET CHILD
BEVERLY BARTON

SILHOUETTE *Desire*

Published by Silhouette Books

America's Publisher of Contemporary Romance

 **SILHOUETTE BOOKS**

ISBN 0-373-76203-8

HIS SECRET CHILD

Printed in U.S.A.

Books by Beverly Barton

Silhouette Desire

Yankee Lover #580
Lucky in Love #628
Out of Danger #662
Sugar Hill #687
Talk of the Town #711
The Wanderer #766
Cameron #796
The Mother of My Child #831
Nothing But Trouble #881
The Tender Trap #1047
A Child of Her Own #1077
†*His Secret Child* #1203

*The Protectors
†3 Babies for 3 Brothers

Silhouette Intimate Moments

This Side of Heaven #453
Paladin's Woman #515
Lover and Deceiver #557
The Outcast #614
Defending His Own #670
Guarding Jeannie #688
Blackwood's Woman #707
Roarke's Wife #807
*A Man Like
   Morgan Kane* #819
Gabriel Hawk's Lady #830
Emily and the Stranger #860
Lone Wolf's Lady #877

Silhouette Books

36 Hours
Nine Months

BEVERLY BARTON

has been in love with romance since her grandfather gave her an illustrated book of *Beauty and the Beast*. An avid reader since childhood, she began writing at the age of nine and wrote short stories, poetry, plays and novels throughout high school and college. After marriage to her own "hero" and the births of her daughter and son, she chose to be a full-time homemaker, a.k.a. wife, mother, friend and volunteer.

When she returned to writing, she joined Romance Writers of America and helped found the Heart of Dixie chapter in Alabama. Since the release of her first Silhouette book in 1990, she has won the GRW Maggie Award and the National Readers' Choice Award and has been a RITA finalist. Beverly considers writing romance books a real labor of love. Her stories come straight from the heart, and she hopes that all the strong and varied emotions she invests in her books will be felt by everyone who reads them.

To Paula Detmer Riggs,
with whom I share secrets that only our souls know.

One

Caleb Bishop dropped his suitcase on the front porch. He was home. Funny thing was, this old house in Crooked Oak didn't seem much like home anymore. He'd left at eighteen and had been back only twice—his grandfather's funeral and his sister's wedding.

He wouldn't be here now if there was anyplace else on earth where he could hide away and lick his wounds.

Giving the old wooden porch swing a nudge with his hand, he watched it sway back and forth and remembered the summer he'd helped his grandfather build the swing. At that time his brother Jake had already been gone six years and they'd had no idea where he was. Hank had been in the army for a year, and their tomboy sister Tallie had been only fourteen. He had just turned sixteen and his prized possession was a black 1980 Camaro, the car he later wrecked, the night after his high school graduation.

Turning around to face the house, Caleb reached under the cushion in the wooden rocker to the left of the swing.

He clasped the house key in his hand. Shaking his head, he grinned. Some things never changed, especially in a place like Crooked Oak, Tennessee. Maybe that was the reason he'd come home, back to where life was uncomplicated and the people were basically good.

Using his right hand, he inserted the key in the lock, then turned the doorknob. The damn thing wouldn't open. Was it stuck? Had Tallie changed the lock and just forgotten and left the old key under the cushion? Balling his hand into a fist, he gritted his teeth and cursed. Switching to his left hand, he turned the key again and heard a distinct *click*, then he grabbed the doorknob and rotated it. The door opened. Caleb grunted.

The simple things were what bothered him the most because they were the things he often forgot he could no longer accomplish the way he used to. Unlocking a door should be easy, and it was, really. Just not quite as easy as it had been when his right hand had worked properly.

Caleb stared at his hand, then ran his gaze up the length of his disabled arm. Sometimes he wished they'd just sawed the damn thing off. What good was it to him, hanging there, the whole thing, from armpit to fingertips, practically useless to him?

He kicked the door open wide, picked up his suitcase and stepped into the living room. Home sweet home.

A woman's voice, singing a few lines from an old Lionel Richie hit, drifted through the house. Caleb froze. Who the hell was here? Not Tallie. She was living in Nashville now and married to the governor of the state. Then who could it be? No one else knew he was coming home.

Maybe Tallie had hired a local woman to come in and freshen up the place. Caleb set down his suitcase, retrieved the key, then closed the door and walked toward the sound of the woman's voice.

"Hello?" he called. "Who's there?" He hoped whomever Tallie had hired knew how to keep her mouth shut.

He really needed a few days of peace and quiet before word leaked out that the hometown celebrity had returned. He was Crooked Oak's most famous citizen. Caleb Bishop, star pitcher for the Atlanta Braves. At least, that's who he had been. But not anymore.

"Oh," she gasped. "I—I didn't expect you until to-night."

She stood in the arched opening between the living room and dining room, a tall, rawboned blonde wearing a pair of overalls. He guessed her age to be around thirty. Her clean-scrubbed face looked vaguely familiar.

"I'm sorry," she said. "I meant to be out of here before you arrived. Tallie asked me to air out the place and bring in some supplies. She told me that you probably wouldn't want to go into town for a few days."

She looked at him with wide, round blue eyes. All the while she kept babbling away, apparently trying to explain her presence. It was obvious he made her nervous.

"It's all right." Caleb looked her over from head to toe. She was a big woman, strong and sturdy and rather attractive in a plain, wholesome way. He was sure he knew her. Why the hell couldn't he remember who she was? "I'm glad Tallie hired you to take care of things. Will you be coming by a couple of times a week?"

"I beg your pardon?" Seeming surprised by his question, she stared at him with those big, beautiful blue eyes.

"Didn't my sister hire you to take care of things around here for me?"

"Oh." Her face reddened, completely obliterating the tiny smattering of freckles across her cheekbones. "Tallie didn't hire me. She and I are friends. I got the place ready for you as a favor to her."

Suddenly, he remembered. "Sheila Hanley! My God, I didn't recognize you at first." Sheila Hanley, the girl who'd made it possible for him to pass twelfth grade English, graduate from high school and accept a college baseball scholarship. How could he not have recognized her? She'd grown older and slimmer, and her once-dark blond hair was now sun-streaked, but she hadn't changed that much. The biggest change was in her dark blue eyes. He didn't remember them being so cool and void of emotion.

"Sheila Vance," she corrected him.

"Oh, yeah, that's right. You married Dan Vance and had a kid, didn't you?" Caleb racked his brain trying to remember anything Tallie might have told him about Sheila over the years. "Sorry about Dan. He was a good man. I always liked him. You and Mike took over his share of the business after he died, didn't you? How's Mike doing these days? Your brother was a real pal when we were growing up."

"Mike's fine. He's remarried and expecting his first child. He and I recently bought out Tallie's share of the business. The garage and tow truck are all ours." Sheila nodded toward the kitchen. "There's a barbecue plate for your supper and I brought in enough supplies to last a week. I changed the linens on the bed in your old room and—"

"Thanks, Sheila, I appreciate all you've done." When he took a step toward her, she backed away.

"You're welcome. I—I'll let myself out the back door." She turned to walk away from him.

Caleb called out to her. "Wait."

She halted, but didn't face him.

"I'm sorry I didn't recognize you at first," he said.

"That's all right. We've both changed a lot in twelve years."

"Why didn't I see you at Gramps's funeral or Tallie's wedding?" Sheila was one of his sister's best friends. He couldn't understand her absence at the only two family events that had been important enough to bring him home.

"I was there, Caleb. You just don't remember. No reason you should. You flew in and right back out the day of your grandfather's funeral. I never got a chance to speak to you." Turning slowly, Sheila faced Caleb. "And the day Tallie got married, you arrived late. Besides, I don't think you could see anyone except your girlfriend that day. You couldn't keep your eyes off her."

The mere mention of Kimberly knotted Caleb's stomach. He closed his eyes, trying to blot out the pain, but Kimberly's face flashed through his mind. Brown eyes. Large, laughing mouth. Delicate body. She was the most beautiful thing he'd ever seen. He'd been crazy about her. And he'd killed her.

Noticing the sorrow in Caleb's black eyes, Sheila regretted that she'd said anything about the woman he had loved and lost. "I'm sorry, I wasn't thinking when I—"

"It's okay," Caleb said. "Kimberly died nearly a year ago. I should be able to handle talking about her. Besides, you're right. When I brought her home with me to Tallie's wedding, she was the only woman I could see."

"She was very beautiful," Sheila told him. "Everyone thought so. You two made a striking pair. A perfect couple." She would never forget how ugly and insignificant she'd felt when she'd watched them together—Caleb and the delicately slender supermodel who had been his latest live-in lover at the time. They'd both been absolutely perfect in face and form and so totally "right" as a couple.

"We're not so perfect anymore, are we?" Caleb rubbed his aching right arm. "Kim's dead and I'm... I'm useless."

Somewhere deep inside Sheila existed the young girl who had once adored Caleb Bishop, a foolishly naive girl who would have done anything for him—and had. Now the remnants of that innocent teenager spiraled up from the depths of Sheila's heart in sympathy and concern for this man who stood in front of her, a man who was little more than a stranger now.

"Just because your baseball career is over doesn't mean you're useless." Her calm voice had a sharp, judgmental tone. "You're still rich, handsome and intelligent. There are a lot of people who'd give anything to have that much."

Knowing full well that Sheila had just put him in his place, Caleb chuckled. Being able to laugh at himself felt damn good. He hadn't been able to do that in a long time. Usually when someone talked to him as plainly as Sheila had just done, he bit their head off.

"Now I remember that your honesty was one of the things I always liked about you," he said. "You never played games the way so many girls did. You always said what you thought and you sure as hell gave me more than one tongue-lashing that last senior semester when you tutored me in English."

"I'm surprised you remember anything about those months. They were so long ago." A lifetime ago, Sheila thought. Danny's lifetime.

"Despite the fact that I didn't recognize you when I first walked in, I do remember you and those months when you pounded some sense into my brain. I know, better than anyone, that without your help I never would have graduated and gone on to play baseball in college. I owed you a lot, Sheila, and I never repaid you in any way."

"Your grandfather paid me to tutor you. It was a job I did for other kids who needed help. And you took me out to celebrate after graduation. Back then, that meant a lot to a girl like me. You could have had a date with any girl in the whole county."

Sheila silently chastised herself for reminding him of that night. Why had she? For her sake and Danny's sake, she should hope he never remembered any of the details. If he did, he might find out the truth she'd kept hidden from him for twelve years.

"God, that was some night, wasn't it? I was leaving for the summer a week after graduation and I was really full of myself because I'd won a baseball scholarship."

"Yeah, it was some night," Sheila said. "But I'm afraid

I can't hang around and reminisce anymore. I've got to get home. Danny has practice…'' She stopped talking mid-sentence, realizing that she shouldn't be discussing her son with Caleb Bishop.

"Danny? Is that your son?" Caleb asked. "You named him after his father, huh?"

"Yes, Danny's my son." Sheila backed into the kitchen. "I hope you'll be comfortable here. Enjoy your supper. And if you need anything, give me a call. I left my number on a pad by the phone." She nodded toward the small table in the living room.

"I wish you could stay. I…" He'd been about to tell her that he was lonely and needed someone to talk to, to listen and understand. Someone even to fuss at him and argue with him. But Sheila had her own life. A child. A home. A business. She'd hardly have any time to waste on him. After all, what was he to her? Nothing more than her friend Tallie's big brother.

Don't give in to that sad, wounded, lost look in his eyes, Sheila told herself. Don't involve yourself in Caleb's life. If you do, you'll just get hurt again. And this time, it won't be only you who will suffer. It'll be Danny, too.

"I've got to go," she told him, but she lingered, drawn to him now, as she had been long ago.

He'd been a devastatingly handsome young man; some had even called him pretty. But Sheila had always thought Caleb was too masculine to be a pretty boy, despite his perfect features. He was, in some ways, better looking now since he had matured. He'd always been big, but the gangly form of his youth had disappeared and left in its stead a sturdy, muscular body that made a woman wonder what it would be like to be possessed by all that masculine power.

Caleb studied the woman in front of him. "Thanks for everything you did. Getting the old homestead ready for me. Airing out the place and bringing over my supper was nice of you." He had always liked Sheila, had even thought of her a few times over the years. She'd always had a gentle strength he'd never known in any other woman. He didn't think he'd ever known any other female, except his sister Tallie, whom he'd genuinely liked. Oh, he'd adored a lot of women, seduced more than his share, had even been head over heels in love a couple of times, but he didn't think he'd *liked* any of those women. Not even Kim. She had been as big a phony as he'd been. Her whole world had revolved around herself, just the way his world had revolved around him.

"I have to go, Caleb." Sheila realized that she needed to break eye contact with him, to end the spell his pleading gaze had cast over her.

"Yeah, I know. Go on. I'm fine. I'll settle in, eat my supper and go to bed early."

"Give Tallie a call and let her know you made it home okay."

"You'd think she was my mother instead of my kid sister, the way she's hovered over me since the accident."

"She loves you, that's why."

For one brief moment Caleb thought he saw a flicker of some deep emotion on Sheila's face. Surely after all these years, she didn't still care about him. Twelve years ago she'd had a crush on him and despite the fact she hadn't been his type back then, he'd been flattered by her shy adoration.

"I'll see you around," Sheila said, her voice steady and calm. "Take care of yourself."

She made it to the back door before Caleb caught up with her. He grabbed her shoulder. She froze. He turned her slowly to face him. "To most of the people around here, I'm a local hero, and that's going to make it difficult for me to fit in. I need a friend who isn't intimidated by the fact that I was the star pitcher for the Atlanta Braves. I need you, Sheila."

No, her mind screamed. *Yes,* her heart pleaded. "I'm sorry, Caleb. I can't. I..."

He massaged her shoulder, felt her shudder. Caleb wasn't sure exactly why it was suddenly so important to him to renew his old friendship with Sheila, but it was. Maybe she reminded him of good times, of being very young and— Who was he kidding? He was a man who'd been without a woman for more than a year. He'd spent months in the hospital after the accident and not until recently had he been able to even dress himself. Sheila Hanley Vance might not be a beauty, but there was something about her that made him want to run his hands over her big, sturdy body, made him want to lift her onto the wooden table in the middle of the kitchen and slide between her legs.

Even if he hadn't recognized her when he'd first seen her tonight, his body had remembered hers. She'd been a virgin that night twelve years ago, but she'd been eager and wild and as willing as any woman he'd ever taken.

There had been too many women in his life, especially when he'd been younger. He couldn't even remember some of their names. But Sheila had been different. Different because he had genuinely liked her.

"Is there some man in your life who would object to our being friends?" he asked.

"I date occasionally," she told him. "But I'm not involved with anyone right now."

"Then why—"

"Because I don't have room for you in my life, Caleb Bishop." Pulling out of his grasp, she turned her back to him and opened the door. "I don't have time to be the kind of friend you need. But there are dozens of women in Crooked Oak who'd be glad to be your friend."

She walked out onto the back porch, but before she could close the door, Caleb grabbed her around the waist and twirled her so that she faced him. He jerked her up against him, circled the back of her neck with his big left hand and brought his mouth forcefully down on hers.

She tried to fight the urge to melt into him, to give herself over to his assault, but the effort failed. She responded to his brutal kiss with equal fury, opening her mouth to accept his thrusting tongue.

This mad dizziness was a unique sensation. Sheila hadn't felt anything like it since the last time Caleb had kissed her. The night she had given him her virginity and her heart—and he had given her Danny.

Suddenly remembering her son—Caleb's son, the child he didn't know he had fathered—Sheila ended the kiss and shoved against Caleb's chest.

Cupping her hip, he pressed her into his arousal and groaned deep in his throat. "We were friends, even lovers for one night. There's no reason why we couldn't be again, since neither of us is attached."

Pushing him away, Sheila glared at Caleb. Her heart wept for what could have been—and for what could never be. But she looked at him squarely, her eyes dry, her face void of emotion. Calmly and without anger, she said, "When you first walked into your old home a few minutes ago, you didn't even recognize me. I doubt you've given me, our former friendship or our one-night stand a thought in twelve years. I'm not one of your beautiful, sophisticated women, Caleb. I'm a widow and a mother, living in a little town in Tennessee. I'm not in the market for a brief affair with the hometown hero."

She turned and walked away, out into the yard and down the gravel road at the side of the house. Standing on the back porch, Caleb watched her until she was out of sight. With every soft, natural sway of her womanly hips, his whole body throbbed with need.

Sheila Hanley Vance had just put him in his place again. Something a woman hadn't done in a long time. Actually not since Sheila had slapped his face the first time he'd kissed her. Women didn't say no to Caleb Bishop, star athlete. Beautiful women, sexy women, rich women threw themselves at him on a regular basis. And now here he'd just been turned down by a big, rawboned, rather plain woman wearing a pair of faded overalls.

Despite the aching need in his body, he laughed loud and hard and long. Hell, Sheila was right. There had to be a couple of dozen women in Crooked Oak who'd jump at the chance to go to bed with him if he needed a woman so damn bad. But as much as he'd enjoy female companionship, he needed his privacy even more. At least for a while. Until he'd come to terms with being back home. Until he decided what he was going to do with the rest of his life, now that his major league career was over.

Sooner or later he would get tired of being alone out here. Sooner or later he'd want female companionship even more than he did right now. But the thought of bedding some starry-eyed *fan* didn't appeal to him. Just once, he'd like to make love to a woman who genuinely cared about him, the way Sheila had cared about him all those years ago.

Sheila increased her pace as soon as she rounded the bend in the road and knew that Caleb could no longer see her. Breaking into a run, she raced homeward, wanting to put as much distance between Caleb Bishop and her as she possibly could.

She hadn't meant for him to find her at his house; she'd meant to be long gone before he arrived. Now, as the March wind whipped loose strands of her hair against her cheeks and her heartbeat roared in her ears, tears that she could not—would not—shed lodged in her throat.

Breathless and damp with perspiration, she bounded up the steps to her front porch. Slumping down on the top step, she covered her face with her hands and rested her elbows on her knees.

When Tallie had phoned from Nashville to ask her to open up the house for Caleb's return, she'd wanted to tell her friend no. But she couldn't refuse. What excuse could she have possibly given Tallie? Even though Tallie had known Sheila had a crush on Caleb twelve years ago, she didn't know anything about that one night they'd spent together. And she didn't know the truth about Danny.

Tallie probably thought she'd play matchmaker and throw Sheila and Caleb together, giving Sheila a chance with the guy she'd been in love with at eighteen. But the last thing Sheila wanted was Caleb Bishop back in Crooked Oak for any length of time.

If Caleb ever found out exactly how old Danny was, if he ever took a good, hard look at her son, he just might start to wonder. A man at loose ends, his once-glamorous and exciting life ended, Caleb was probably searching for something to fill the empty days. But once he came to terms with his disability and had a chance to decide what he wanted to do with the rest of his life, he'd leave Crooked Oak. When he'd left her twelve years ago, she had survived. But she didn't want her son to have to suffer over Caleb Bishop's second departure. Danny had gone through enough when Daniel had died five years ago. He had already lost one father. She wasn't going to run the risk of his accepting Caleb into his life and then losing him, too.

Sheila stood, dusted her hands off on her hips and went inside the small, wooden house she'd lived in with her husband. She heard the television in Danny's room and knew he was watching "Nickleodeon." She allowed her son a great deal of freedom, and with each passing year she let him make more and more of his own decisions. If he was watching TV, that meant he'd finished his homework and was probably ready for dinner. They usually ate around five-thirty during the months when Danny didn't have baseball practice, and it was already past five now.

She walked down the hall and stopped in front of

Danny's open door. Peeping in, she saw him spread out across the bed, his back braced against the headboard. He glanced away from the TV and up at her. He smiled. And for one endless moment Sheila's heart stood still. He had his father's smile. That lazy, smirking grin that curved the left side of his mouth. She was surprised that no one had ever noticed. If Caleb had been around all these years, someone would have put two and two together long ago.

"Hi, Mom. Did you get Tallie's house all fixed up for Caleb?"

"Yes."

"When's he supposed to get here? Sometime tonight?"

"He's already here. He came before I left."

"Did you talk to him? Gosh, Mom, I can't believe that Caleb Bishop is living down the road from us." Danny scooted to the side of the bed and jumped up. "Do you think he'd give me his autograph? The guys at school didn't believe me when I told them that my mom was going to take Caleb Bishop his supper."

Danny rushed across the room, picked up his baseball and leather glove, then tossed the ball into the air and adeptly caught it in the mitt. "Do you think he'd mind giving me some pointers? You could tell him who I am, that Tallie's practically my aunt, since you and she are such good friends."

Sheila grasped her son's shoulder and forced a smile on her face. "We're not going to bother Caleb while he's visiting Crooked Oak. He's come here to recuperate. But if he stays long enough, I'm sure we'll run into him sooner or later."

"Ah, gee, Mom, couldn't I just stop by his house and get his autograph?"

"No, you may not. I don't want you pestering Caleb."

"Asking a famous person for his autograph isn't pestering him."

"Danny Vance, I want you to promise me that you won't go over to Tallie's house and bother Caleb."

"Ah, Mom."

She had to keep Danny and Caleb apart if at all possible. The more they were together, the more likely it would be that someone would notice the similarities between the two. Even Caleb might notice that Danny didn't resemble Daniel Vance in the least. Danny had inherited her blue eyes, but that was all. His black hair and dark complexion were genetic gifts from Caleb, as were his natural athletic abilities.

"I'll tell you what," Sheila said. "Promise me that you won't bother Caleb and I'll make sure you meet him and get his autograph before he leaves Crooked Oak."

"Okay," Danny agreed reluctantly.

"Go wash up and get ready for supper. We're having barbecue."

"Great. Barbecue is my favorite." Danny tossed the ball and glove down on his bed, then raced out of the bedroom and up the hall to the bathroom.

Sheila ran her hand lovingly over the baseball glove she'd given Danny for Christmas. He'd been fascinated with the game since he was a baby, and Daniel had bought him his first ball and bat, both plastic, when he was two.

Daniel had been a good man. A kind husband and a loving father to a child he'd known wasn't his. She still missed him, and knew that Danny did, too. Surviving Caleb Bishop's return would have been so much easier if Daniel were still alive.

But Daniel was gone, and she had no one else to count on except herself. She and she alone would have to find a way to protect herself and her son from a man who could bring them nothing but heartache.

Two

Caleb hit the rewind button on the VCR and cursed himself for a fool. Why the hell had he brought along the tape of last season's final playoffs game—the last baseball game of Caleb Bishop's illustrious career—when watching himself in top form was an excruciating torment?

"You're a glutton for punishment, aren't you, Bishop?" he said to himself. "How many times are you going to watch that damn tape?"

When he stood, he tossed the remote control onto the sofa and headed for the kitchen. His stomach rumbled, as if on cue, the moment he entered the neat, white kitchen. Glancing at the clock on the microwave, he noticed that it was nearly noon. He hadn't eaten a bite since he'd gotten up nearly four hours ago.

For the past ten days he had shut himself off from the rest of the world. Living like a hermit, he hadn't even answered the telephone for the first few days. But Tallie's insistent messages warning him that if he didn't pick up the damn phone before long, she was going to drive down from Nashville and personally kick his butt, encouraged him to make contact with the outside world.

Caleb pulled a box of cereal from an upper cupboard, retrieved the milk from the refrigerator and prepared himself a bowl of cornflakes. The supply of groceries Sheila Vance had brought him was nearly gone. Within a day or two, he'd either have to make a trip into town or ask Sheila to do some shopping for him. He liked the idea of giving Sheila a call. More than once he had stopped himself from contacting her and using any pretense to lure her over to his house. But she'd made it perfectly clear that she wasn't interested in a brief affair. No, she wouldn't be. His instincts told him that Sheila was still the type of girl who'd want a long-term commitment from a guy. And he simply wasn't the kind of man who made a woman promises he couldn't keep.

Just as he downed the last spoonful of soggy flakes, the telephone rang. Damn, why couldn't Tallie leave him alone! He jerked the receiver from the wall hook by the back door and growled into the phone.

"Yeah, what do you want now?"

"And hello to you, too," Hank Bishop said.

"Hank?"

"Yep. Who'd you think it was?"

"Tallie," Caleb replied. "Our little sister is driving me nuts trying to keep tabs on me from Nashville. You'd think with a husband, a baby and duties as first lady of the state, she wouldn't have time to pester the hell out of me."

Hank chuckled, the deep sound reverberating from his chest.

"Well, you know our Tallie. She can't keep her nose out of everybody else's business."

"So, what's up, big brother? Or are you checking on the washed-up has-been, too?"

"You're going to have to stop feeling sorry for yourself

sooner or later," Hank said. "Why don't you do all of us, yourself included, a big favor and make it sooner?"

Caleb snorted. "Humph. Straight to the heart of the matter, as always. You make it sound so easy. Just pick myself up by the bootstraps, dust myself off and do...do what, big brother? I wasn't the smart, straight-arrow type like you. And I wasn't the hell-raising rebel like Jake. All I ever wanted was to play baseball. Since I was just a little kid. Now, that's gone. Forever. And I don't have the slightest idea what to do with the rest of my life."

"How about starting by being grateful you have the rest of your life."

Caleb knew that his older brother meant well, but Hank didn't know what it felt like to have his life out of control, his dreams destroyed and his future uncertain. No, Hank was the type who, no matter what happened, would always take charge and find a way to do the honorable thing. If Hank were in his shoes, he'd already have mapped out a new course for his future. But then, Hank was the smart brother. Caleb was the dumb jock.

"Yeah," Caleb agreed. "I suppose being a pitcher with a useless right arm is better than being dead."

"Are you still moping around the old homestead?" Hank asked. "Haven't you even been into town? I'll bet folks are dying to see you and welcome the local hero back to Crooked Oak. And there's probably more than one cute girl who'd like to ease your loneliness."

Caleb chuckled. There was no point denying his lady-killer reputation, not to his own brother, who knew him better than anyone else alive. "As a matter of fact, I met a rather interesting woman the first day I came back."

"I thought you hadn't left the house."

"This particular woman was here when I arrived. She'd aired out the place, brought in groceries and had my supper waiting for me."

"Are you talking about Tallie's friend? What's her

name? Mike Hanley's kid sister? The one who married Dan Vance?''

"That's the one. Sheila Vance."

"If I remember correctly, I'd say the woman isn't your usual type."

"Maybe I'd like to try something different for a change," Caleb said. "I've had my share of airheaded beauties. Sheila may be a plain Jane, but there's something about her that—"

"It's called quality," Hank said. "Tallie thinks highly of Sheila. Seems she's had it pretty rough, widowed so young and trying to raise a child on her own. Think twice before you use a woman like her to ease your loneliness."

"If you're warning me not to hurt Sheila, save your breath. Tallie's already read me the riot act."

"Good for her." Hank cleared his throat. "Why don't you come up to Virginia and stay with me for a while?"

"I might later on. But for now I just want to stay put to try to figure out who the hell Caleb Bishop is if he's not the star pitcher for the Atlanta Braves."

"You'll figure it out." Hank sighed loud enough for Caleb to hear him.

"Do me a favor, will you? Call our little sister and ask her to leave me alone, at least for a few days."

"Will do. Talk to you in a couple of weeks."

"So long." Caleb hung up the receiver, then glanced out the kitchen window at the vast backyard and thickly wooded area behind the house. If he was a hunter and fisherman, the way Hank was, he could pass the time with a rifle or with a rod and reel. And if he was a hard-living SOB like Jake, he could hit every bar in town and ease some of his frustration in a few fistfights.

But baseball had been his only passion for so many years that he could barely remember ever caring about anything else. As a teenager, the only other thing that had interested him had been his 1980 Camaro—the car he had wrecked, the car Tallie had put back together years later.

Cars. Hmm. Maybe he needed to buy himself a fixer-upper street rod and— Hell, how could he do any work on a car when his right hand was practically useless to him?

Sheila and Mike owned a garage, didn't they? He could stop by and talk to them about helping him find something special—maybe another Camaro—and he could hire them to do most of the work. He could hang around the garage and watch, and occasionally do a few things himself.

Okay, Bishop, admit the truth. You need an excuse to see Sheila Vance again. An excuse she'll buy without any question.

"All right, I admit it," he said out loud to himself. "I don't know why I can't stop thinking about Sheila. Maybe it's because she's so different from the women I've always dated. Maybe it's because winning her over would be a real challenge."

Think twice before you use a woman like her to ease your loneliness. Caleb heard Hank's warning once again.

Sheila was no kid. She was a thirty-year-old widow, not some naive innocent. A pang of guilt hit him square in the gut. *At least not this time,* an inner voice said. Okay. Okay. So Sheila had been a shy bookworm when he'd known her twelve years ago. And yes, he'd been pretty sure she was a virgin the night he made love to her. But it wasn't as if he'd forced himself on her. She'd been more than willing for him to be her first lover.

She was in love with you, you bastard!

But that was then and this is now. Sheila was no starry-eyed, infatuated innocent anymore. If they had a brief affair now, they would meet on equal terms—two lonely people in need of companionship.

Who the hell was he kidding? Sheila Vance was no more in his league now than she'd been when they were eighteen. He had no right to even consider seducing her. But, God help him, he knew that given half a chance he'd take her and to hell with the consequences.

Mike Hanley placed the hot Reuben and fries on the desk in front of his sister. She glanced up from the computer and smiled at him.

"Thanks. I'm starving." She shoved back her chair, stood and headed for the small rest room adjacent to her office.

"Don't you think it's time we talk about it?" Mike said. "You've put me off every time I've brought up the subject."

Leaving the bathroom door open, Sheila washed and dried her hands. "What's there to talk about? Caleb's back in Crooked Oak for a brief visit and when he's pulled his life back together, he'll be gone again."

"Well, it doesn't look like he's in any hurry to leave. He's already been here ten days and hasn't even put in an appearance in town. The natives are getting restless for a good look at the big celebrity."

"I suppose Caleb was the main topic of conversation over at Pete's Café, wasn't he?" Sheila returned to her desk, opened the styrene food container and growled hungrily when she picked up the sandwich.

"Caleb Bishop has been the main topic in town ever since your son told all his buddies that the great man had arrived." Mike sat down on the edge of the battered old wooden desk, reached out and grasped his sister's chin. "Sticking your head in the sand isn't going to work, you know. Crooked Oak is a small town. If Caleb stays—and it looks like he's going to—then sooner or later he and Danny are going to come face-to-face. What happens then?"

Sheila swallowed the delectable mouthful of corned beef. "Nothing happens. There's no reason for Caleb to suspect anything. After all, not a soul in town ever questioned that Daniel was Danny's father. Why should Caleb?''

"Because Caleb is one of four people who knows you and he had sex twelve years ago.'' Mike released her chin. "Have you talked to Susan lately?''

"I've been avoiding her calls,'' Sheila admitted. "I know she's going to do just what you've been doing— torment me.''

"Honey, it's your own conscience that's tormenting you. You're feeling guilty for lying to Danny about his father. And you're scared to death that somehow he and Caleb are going to find out the truth.''

"I won't let that happen.'' Sheila broke a French fry in two. "I will not let Danny get hurt because of my mistakes.''

The telephone rang. Sheila jumped, then glared at the noisy object.

"Want me to get it?'' Mike asked.

"No, of course not.'' Sheila lifted the receiver. "Hanley Garage and Tow Truck Service.''

"Sheila? Have you seen my brother today?''

"Oh, hello, Tallie, how are you?''

Mike's eyes widened and his mouth curved into a smile. "Tell the first lady I said hello. I'm going back to work. Mr. Chapman is coming by in about an hour to pick up his Suburban.''

The minute Mike left the office, Sheila lowered her voice and said, "I haven't seen Caleb since the first evening he got into town. Why would you think I'd seen him today?''

"Well, I talked to him earlier and he promised me that he'd get out for a while this afternoon.''

"What makes you think he'd come to see me?''

"Because he said he planned to stop by the garage and talk to you and Mike about finding him an antique car that the three of you could restore together.''

"Oh!'' Oh, my God! The last thing she wanted—the

very last thing she needed—was a reason to spend any time with Caleb. But if he did come by and hire Mike to help him restore an old car, how could she possibly refuse? What reasonable explanation could she give for not taking his money?

"Look, I can trust you to watch out for Caleb. He's lonely and vulnerable right now," Tallie said. "Without someone to keep close tabs on him, he's liable to let the first pretty face he meets get him into trouble. The last thing he needs is some hero-worshiping fan to get her claws into him."

"What do you expect me to do about it?" Sheila asked. "Besides, if he doesn't ever leave the farm, then it's highly unlikely that some crazed female fan is going to seduce him."

"All I'm asking is that if Caleb needs a little female companionship while he's in town, you provide it for him."

"I'm afraid your idea of companionship and your brother's are two different things. And believe me, I'm not sleeping with your brother as a favor to you."

"Hell's toenails," Tallie said, moaning dramatically. "I don't expect you to. It's just that he's all alone and you're all alone and—"

"I'm not all alone," Sheila told her. "I have family. Danny. Mike and his Christy. And I have dated Pat Lawley a few times recently."

"Pat Lawley? My heavens, Sheila, you're four inches taller than Pat and five years older. I like Pat, but he's hardly the man for you."

"Pat and I are the same height. And he's twenty-seven, which makes him three years younger than I am."

"Doesn't matter. Pat's not right for you."

"You aren't implying that you think Caleb is the right man for me, are you?"

"Well, maybe not. But I do remember a time when you had quite a crush on my brother. If he'd had any sense back then, he would have snapped you up before Dan Vance married you.''

"Tallie!''

"Oh, all right, I'll stop trying to play matchmaker. If you're not interested in Caleb for yourself, then try to find him some nice girl to date while he's in town. And I mean *nice.*''

"I'll see what I can do.''

"Thanks. And give me a call in a few days and let me know how he's doing. Okay?''

"Okay.''

After hanging up the phone, Sheila rested her elbows on the desk and cradled her chin in her cupped hands. If Tallie hadn't been Caleb's sister, she would have told her the truth twelve years ago. When she had discovered she was pregnant, she'd gone straight to Susan Williams, who had been the third member of their friendship triangle. Sheila hadn't wanted to keep the truth from Tallie, but she had convinced Susan and herself that if Tallie knew the child she was carrying belonged to Caleb, then Tallie would tell her brother. And the last thing she'd wanted was to ruin Caleb's big chance to play college baseball.

She might have felt differently about things if Caleb had loved her. But he hadn't. He'd taken her out on graduation night and she'd suspected all along that the date was a repayment for her valuable assistance in helping him pass his final exam. What had started out as a pleasant evening spent with a friend had turned into a passionate night that she had never been able to forget. She had lived off the memory of that one night for twelve years. She had lain in Dan Vance's arms during the intimate moments of their marriage and thought about the night another man had made love to her. And she suspected that Dan had known and had forgiven her for being unable to forget the man who had fathered her child.

A gentle tapping on the open door alerted Sheila of a

potential customer. She looked up to see Caleb Bishop poised in the doorway, his long, lean frame silhouetted by the afternoon sunlight behind him. Her heart skipped a beat. Her stomach fluttered. Damn him for still having such a potent effect on her. Damn him for coming back into her life and unsettling her peaceful existence. And damn him for unwittingly putting Danny's security at risk.

"Hello," he said. "Have you got time for me?"

She wanted to scream no loud and clear. She wanted to tell him to go away and leave her alone, to stop sending her into turmoil with his nearness. But she couldn't say or do anything to alert him that she was afraid of him, that his presence in her life was a danger to both her and her son.

"Sure. What do you need?" She whirled the swivel chair around, shoved it back and stood to face him.

I need you, honey, he wanted to say, but didn't. I need to set you up on that old desk of yours, spread your legs, unzip my jeans and… His thoughts wreaked havoc on his body. His sex enlarged and tightened uncomfortably.

He removed his cap and fiddled with it in his large hands. "I, er, I thought maybe you and Mike could find me an old hot rod to restore. I couldn't do all the work myself—" he raised his limp right arm "—but I thought I might keep the car here and y'all could help me fix it up. It'd give me something to do to pass the time."

"What's the matter? Have you gotten tired of holing up at the farm and feeling sorry for yourself?"

He grinned, that devastatingly cocky grin that countless female fans swooned over. Sheila wanted to shout to the world that he had bestowed that special smile on her years before he'd become a baseball star.

"Yeah, something like that." He took several tentative steps into her office. "So, do you think you can find me a car?"

"I'm sure Mike can, if you tell him what you're looking

for. He's working on a van right now. Why don't you go on out to the garage and talk to him?''

"Do you still tinker around on cars yourself?" he asked. "I remember you were almost as good a mechanic as Tallie.''

"Occasionally I get my hands greasy," she said. "If Mike needs my help. But mostly I handle the office and take part of the tow truck calls.''

"I remember when Gramps and Dan first went into business together. It was right after Gramps's first heart attack and the doctor told him he couldn't work at the factory any longer. Dan had been recently widowed and left his job in Chattanooga to come home to Crooked Oak and put his life back together. Sure never thought he'd wind up marrying one of Tallie's friends.''

"Dan was a good man and we had a good marriage, despite the difference in our ages. I still miss him terribly.''

"Yeah, I guess you do." Caleb's body relaxed enough that he felt comfortable moving in a little closer to Sheila. "But at least he left you with a child. I imagine having Dan's son makes living without him easier.''

Myriad emotions tightened Sheila's chest. For one brief moment she couldn't breathe. Her instant reaction to Caleb's comment was fury. She wanted to pound his chest with her fists and tell him that her child was his son, not Daniel's.

A long, seemingly endless moment of silence strung out between them. Say something, Sheila told herself. Say something before he wonders why you're reacting this way. But before she could think of an appropriate response, a woman's soft voice called from the doorway.

"Hi." Smiling directly at Sheila, Donna Fields curled her small hand and waved her fingers in greeting. "I stopped by to see if my car's ready.''

Glad for any interruption, Sheila breathed a sigh of relief. "Oh, Donna, come on in.''

The elegantly slender woman, a mane of mahogany red hair falling around her shoulders, entered the small office. She halted beside Caleb, who had turned and openly admired the woman's physical beauty.

"Hello," Donna said. "I don't think we've met. Are you a customer or a friend?"

Caleb reached out and took Donna's hand, gave it a lingering squeeze, then grinned devilishly, flirtatiously. And the Green-eyed Monster soared inside Sheila like a jet plane in flight. Did the man have to try to charm every woman he met?

"I'm an old friend and a potential customer," Caleb replied. "Caleb Bishop, at your service, pretty lady."

"Caleb Bishop?" Donna practically gushed with enthusiasm and pleasure. "Tallie's brother. The baseball player." She pumped Caleb's hand. "I've heard so much about the Bishop brothers from Tallie that I feel as if I know all three of you."

"I'm sure she told you that I'm the handsome one." Caleb's smile widened. "By the way, how do you know Tallie? You weren't one of her high school friends. Believe me, I'd remember if you were."

Oh, yeah, Sheila thought. *Her he would remember.*

Donna laughed, obviously charmed by the man who still held her hand. "Actually, I met Tallie when I was dating Peyton." She chucked at his puzzled expression. "Oh, there wasn't anything serious between your brother-in-law and me. We were just friends."

Sheila rose from the chair, squared her broad shoulders and stood beside Donna. Might as well let Caleb get a good look at the two of us, side-by-side, get the comparison over with and come to the conclusion that any man would—that Donna Fields was a beautiful desirable woman and Sheila Vance was a big, plain country girl.

"Your car's ready," Sheila said. "I've got your bill."

Donna rummaged in her purse, pulled out a credit card

and handed it to Sheila. "I'd love to stay and chat, but I have an evening class, so I have to rush back to Marshallton for a dinner date with a colleague."

"We'll have to get together soon." Sheila processed the bill, then returned the card to Donna. She pulled a set of keys off a nearby hook. "Here's your keys. Your Corvette's parked in the side lot."

Donna took the keys, gave Sheila a quick hug and whispered in her ear, "Is Susan pregnant yet?"

"Not yet," Sheila replied softly. "Keep your fingers crossed. She and Lowell are going in for some tests next week."

Donna shook her head, then turned to Caleb. "Nice to have finally met one of Tallie's brothers."

"Would you be interested in seeing more of one of Tallie's brothers?" Caleb asked.

"Oh, that's a tempting offer, but I'm afraid I'll have to decline. You see, I'm taking a group of my students from the junior college to England during spring break and I'm going to be terribly busy from now until we leave."

"Maybe when you get back."

"Maybe. If you're still in Crooked Oak."

Caleb watched the strikingly lovely redhead's departure, every male instinct within him admiring the sway of her shapely hips.

"Donna's a beautiful woman, isn't she?" Sheila commented.

Caleb suddenly realized that Sheila had witnessed his practiced come-on to Donna. Damn! When it came to pretty women, he seemed powerless to stop himself from flirting. Sometimes the flirting led to other things, but more often than not, it didn't. However, Sheila would probably judge his actions as those of a philandering jock. After all, he did have the reputation, didn't he? And if he were completely honest with himself, he'd have to admit that the reputation had been fairly earned.

"Yeah, she is beautiful," Caleb said, then turned his attention to Sheila. "So...do you think I should ask her out when she gets back from England?"

"That's entirely up to you," Sheila said.

"What kind of woman is she?"

"A very nice lady."

"Too nice for me?"

"I didn't say that."

"Do you think we'd make a good pair?" he asked.

"In some ways," Sheila said. "Just like you, Donna isn't interested in a commitment. She dates, but she never gets serious about anyone."

"A woman after my own heart." Caleb chuckled. "So Donna likes to play around and—"

"She's a widow who's still in love with her husband. She dates, but she doesn't *play* around, so if you want a sex partner—and I'm sure you do—then Donna's probably the wrong choice."

"What about you, Sheila? Are you a woman who's still in love with her husband?"

I was never in love with Daniel Vance. But I can hardly tell you that fact, any more than I can tell you that Danny is your son or that you're the man I fell in love with when I was just a foolish teenage girl.

"A part of me will always love Daniel." *And I will always be grateful to him for marrying me and giving your son a father.* "But, no, I'm not in love with him."

"Mmm. So, if Mike can find me a car, would you be interested in helping me fix it up?"

"Me? I don't think so. But I'm sure, if the price is right, Mike will help you."

"Why not you?"

Caleb studied Sheila Vance closely. A slight pink flush stained her cheeks. He grinned. His blatant survey obviously embarrassed her.

She was as different from Donna Fields as an oak tree

from a red maple. Donna was breathtaking, colorful and delicately feminine. Sheila was strength and simplicity and looked like the type of woman who could plow a field, fight off a band of renegade natives and give birth—all in the same day.

"Let's just say that I'm not interested, okay?" She had no intention of being one of Caleb Bishop's pastimes while he was visiting Crooked Oak. She wasn't going to volunteer to amuse him for the next couple of weeks, until Donna got back from England or until some other pretty girl caught his eye.

"You're a hard-hearted woman, Sheila Vance."

"I'm a—"

"Hey, Mom. Practice was great. Pat said I'm going to be the Bulldogs's star pitcher this year." Danny Vance raced into the office, a wide, warm smile, identical to his father's, spread across his face.

Sheila's heart missed a beat. Damn, she'd lost track of time. Why hadn't she remembered that Pat Lawley was going to drop Danny by the garage after Little League practice today?

"Did he? That's wonderful, Danny." Sheila forced a smile to her lips. Well, the inevitable had happened. Caleb and Danny were in the same room together. And strangely enough, the world hadn't come to an end. Yet.

"So, this must be your son," Caleb said.

"Yes, this is Danny." Sheila grasped her child's shoulders and turned him around to meet the one man on earth she'd assumed he would never meet. "Danny, this is Caleb Bishop."

"Wow wee, Caleb Bishop!" Danny jerked out of his mother's grasp and rushed over to Caleb. "Man, this is great. Just wait till I tell the guys that I met Caleb Bishop. Right here in my mom and uncle Mike's garage. And Pat. He's a big fan of yours, too. Pat Lawley's our coach. We're the Bulldogs. You ought to come to a game. You'd—"

"Danny, slow down," Sheila said. "You're talking Mr. Bishop to death."

"Yeah, sorry." Danny bowed his head sheepishly. Smiling closemouth, he cut his glance in a sideways gesture she'd seen Caleb make time and again when he was being repentant. "I'd like your autograph, Mr. Bishop. I've got a brand-new ball. Do you think you could sign it for me?"

"Call me Caleb. And I'd be glad to drop by your house any time and sign that new ball."

"How about tonight?" Danny lifted his head and flashed Caleb a brilliant smile. "You could come to dinner. Tonight's pot roast. Mom put it in the Crock-Pot early this morning. She's a great cook and—"

"Danny!" Sheila cautioned him again. "Mr. Bishop…Caleb may already have plans for dinner."

The boy gazed pleadingly at the man and Sheila's heart ached for her son. A boy who missed the only father he'd ever known. A boy who had found a role model in a star athlete.

"Sorry," Danny said.

"As a matter of fact, I don't have any plans." Caleb clasped the boy's shoulder and smiled down at him. "And I'd love to eat some of your mama's pot roast tonight." He glanced over Danny's head and made eye contact with Sheila.

"We eat a little later, now that Little League season has begun," she said. "Come by around six-thirty."

"Thanks," Caleb said. "I'll go talk to Mike about finding me a car." He focused on Danny momentarily. "See you tonight, slugger."

The moment Caleb left the office, Danny jumped up and down, screeching the way only an eleven-year-old boy could.

"Caleb Bishop is coming to my house for dinner tonight! *The* Caleb Bishop. Holy cow, Mom, I'm going to be the envy of every guy at school tomorrow."

Yes, Caleb Bishop was coming to their house for dinner tonight. And she would have to watch them together— Caleb and Danny, father and son—and pretend that everything was normal. Right or wrong, no matter what, her first obligation was to her son. She had to protect him at all costs. Caleb didn't matter. She didn't matter. And any feelings she still had for the man were unimportant.

She could not allow Caleb to become a part of their lives and then walk away from them, as she was sure he would do. She might be willing to risk her heart again for the pleasure of being with Caleb one more time. But she would never put Danny's security and happiness at risk. Not even for Caleb.

Three

———

"You really didn't have to agree to Danny's request to invite Tanner and Devin over here to meet you tonight," Sheila said, placing the iced tea glasses in the top compartment of the dishwasher.

"I know I didn't." Caleb handed her the stack of dirty dishes he had removed from the kitchen table. "But why shouldn't I? I've got plenty of time on my hands and I think it means a lot to Danny."

"Oh, you have no idea." She arranged the plates neatly in a row in the bottom compartment. "My son is one of your biggest fans, and that's saying quite a lot, considering you're the idol of every male in Crooked Oak—boy, teenager and man."

"Did I thank you for the delicious dinner?" he asked.

Caleb moved in behind Sheila as she leaned over the sink and filled the Crock-Pot with warm, soapy water. She felt him, although he didn't actually touch her. The heat of his body. The power of his masculinity. The strength of his presence. When she turned to face him, he was close. Too close. She stepped back in an effort to escape his nearness. Her hips pressed into the counter edge.

"Yes, you thanked me," she said. "Twice."

"Just shows how much I enjoyed having dinner with you…and your son."

"I imagine it's a new experience for you, having dinner with a woman and her child." Sheila took a deep breath and sidestepped Caleb, moving to his left.

He grabbed her arm, his hold tight but gentle. "You didn't want me here tonight, Sheila. Why?"

"I have no idea what you're talking about. You're Tallie's brother and Danny's idol. Why wouldn't you be welcome in my home?"

"That's what I'm asking you." Reaching out with his fingertips, he smoothed back an errant strand of hair that had fallen over her right eye.

Their gazes met and locked for a brief moment and Sheila prayed that what she felt didn't show plainly in her eyes. Caleb was right. She hadn't wanted him in her home tonight, or any other night for that matter.

She pulled out of his grasp, hurried out of the kitchen and into the hallway. If she didn't give him an answer to his question, he was going to wonder what she was trying so hard to hide. And what reasonable explanation, other than the complete truth, could she give him for not wanting him in her life?

The sound of Danny's voice jerked her quickly from her thoughts.

"Yeah, Tanner, he's here right now and he's going to stay until my bedtime," Danny said. "He's going to autograph my baseball and if I ask him to, he might sign yours and Devin's, too."

Sheila paused outside her son's bedroom door. It had been a long time since she'd seen Danny so happy and excited. How could she run Caleb away without breaking

Danny's heart? But if she allowed Caleb to become Danny's buddy, what then? The potential for disaster was too great. Sooner or later, Caleb might figure out the truth. All he had to do was ask Danny when his birthday was.

Covering her mouth with her hands, Sheila bit back a cry of despair. What was she going to do?

Caleb followed her out into the hallway, halted at her side and glanced into the bedroom where Danny lay sprawled out on the bed, the telephone glued to his ear.

"He thinks my mom is a great cook," Danny said. "He ate second helpings of everything. And guess what? Bread pudding with sunshine sauce is his favorite dessert just like it is mine!"

"You've got a great kid there," Caleb whispered as he lowered his head enough so that his lips almost touched her ear.

She closed her eyes, praying that when she spoke her voice wouldn't quiver. Her heart beat rapidly. Her stomach fluttered wildly. It just wasn't fair that Caleb could make her feel this way when no other man ever had.

"Yes, I know. Danny is a wonderful boy." She tried not to notice that Caleb had slipped his arm around her waist or that her traitorous body tingled with excitement. Oh, dear God, all he had to do was touch her and she went weak in the knees.

And weak in the head, too! she reprimanded herself. Get a grip, girl. Don't let him do this to you. Hell, don't do it to yourself. You know better.

"Caleb, I appreciate your being so nice to Danny and accepting his invitation to dinner and—" She glanced over her shoulder and the moment he smiled at her, the bottom dropped out of her stomach. "And signing autographs for him and his friends, but...well, I just don't want Danny to think...to assume—"

Caleb pulled her to the opposite end of the hall, near the

living room, then gently eased her up against the wall. His big body hovered over hers. She swallowed hard.

"You don't want Danny to think—to assume—what?" Caleb asked.

"He lost his father five years ago and even though Mike and he are pals, what Danny wants more than anything is a dad of his own." She hesitated momentarily, allowing Caleb to absorb her words and hopefully come to the right conclusion.

"You think Danny might see me as a father figure? Is that what's got you so worried? You don't want Danny getting too close to me and maybe trying to emulate me? You really don't approve of me, do you, Sheila?"

Oh, great! Hunky-dory great! Typical man, he'd misunderstood.

"I don't approve or disapprove of you. That's not what I was trying to say."

"Then maybe you'd better spell it out for me."

"All right." She squared her shoulders and glared directly into his dark brown eyes. "I don't want you hanging around so much that Danny becomes too attached to you, that he starts thinking of you as a substitute dad. Somebody who'll be in his life for the long haul. If he becomes too fond of you, it'll break his heart when you leave Crooked Oak."

Caleb took a step backward, putting a couple of feet between them and allowing Sheila to move into the living room. He stood there in the hallway and thought about what she'd just told him. If for one minute he'd ever really thought about Danny's situation, he would have realized the danger in spending too much time with the kid. He'd been a fatherless boy himself once. And although his cold, stern grandfather had tried to be a supportive parent, Gramps hadn't been his real father. Hell, he couldn't even remember what his own father looked like. Jake and Hank had been old enough to retain memories of their parents, but he'd been a toddler and Tallie an infant when they'd lost their folks.

Danny barreled out of his bedroom and down the hall, screeching to a halt right in front of Caleb. "The guys will be over in a few minutes. Tanner's dad is going to bring them. Mr. Finch is dying to meet you."

Caleb ruffled Danny's wavy black hair and grinned. The last thing on earth he wanted to do was hurt this boy, to disappoint him in any way. Strange thing was, that for some reason he could see himself in Sheila's son. Danny was tall and lanky—all arms and legs—the way he'd been as a kid. And the boy loved baseball with a passion that bordered on obsession, just as he did. And Danny was a fatherless boy in need of a role model. He'd been there himself and had experienced every aspect of being the only kid on the team without a dad. His grandfather had been an old man with a bad heart, and although he'd come to all the games, he'd never coached or managed one of Caleb's Little League teams the way so many fathers did. Caleb could remember being Danny's age and promising himself that when he had a son, he'd coach the boy's team.

"Danny, you know that I'm going to be in Crooked Oak for just a few months, don't you? I'm not moving back here permanently. Once I sort out what to do with my life now that my major league career is over, I'll be leaving."

Danny stared at Caleb with wide, expressive blue eyes identical to his mother's. "Yeah, sure. I know."

Caleb glanced over Danny's shoulder, into the living room, directing his gaze at Sheila. She smiled weakly and nodded her head.

"I want us to be friends and…well, after I leave town, I'll keep in touch. But…I, er…"

Danny narrowed his eyes, his stare questioning Caleb. "Me and Caleb Bishop friends. Hey, I like the sound of that."

Caleb gripped Danny's shoulder. "I like the sound of that, too."

He thought their little talk had gone well, that he'd set the record straight and eased Sheila's mind. Danny was a bright kid. He understood that Caleb wouldn't be a permanent fixture in his life. Maybe now, Sheila would stop worrying.

He could be Danny's friend without giving the boy any false hopes about him becoming his substitute father, couldn't he? And he and Sheila could renew their old friendship and temporarily ease each other's loneliness, without any permanent ties.

Caleb waited on the front porch while Sheila checked to make sure Danny was asleep. She had put her son to bed three times since his two young buddies had left, and each time he'd thought of just one more thing to tell Caleb.

"This is the last thing, I promise, Mom," the boy had said ten minutes ago. "Caleb, would you come and watch us practice tomorrow? We'll be over behind the grammar school, in Old Man Pickens's field. That's where the Bulldogs always practice."

"Danny!" Sheila had scolded.

"I might drop by for a few minutes," Caleb had replied. "But don't mention it to any of the other guys just in case I don't make it."

Sheila swung open the front door and joined Caleb on the porch.

"He's down for the count," she said. "He's asleep and this time he isn't faking it."

Caleb sat in the porch swing. He knew he should get in his car and drive home instead of lingering, trying to prolong the evening. He dreaded going back to the old homestead alone. He was a man accustomed to company, to being around teammates and fans and—until this past year when he'd been recuperating from the accident—he'd seldom been without a female companion.

"I hope you don't mind that I told Danny I might stop by his practice tomorrow."

She hesitated a couple of seconds before she replied, "No, I don't mind. He would have been terribly disappointed if you'd said no. I think he'd already told Devin and Tanner that he was going to ask you to come by."

"I promise to play it cool with him," Caleb said. "He's a pretty smart boy. He understands that my stay in Crooked Oak is only temporary."

Feeling a sudden chill at his words, Sheila rubbed her hands up and down her arms. "It's cool, isn't it, for springtime?"

"Come sit by me and I'll warm you up," he said, his tone teasing.

He'd like to warm her up, melt that frosty exterior and see just how hot Sheila could get. He remembered a passionate young girl who had come alive in his arms. Was that fire and passion still alive in her, just waiting to be unleashed? She had told him there was no one special in her life, so that had to mean she was celibate because unless Sheila had changed a great deal, she'd never indulge in casual sex.

"Aren't you leaving?" she asked. "It's ten-thirty. Past my bedtime. We're early risers around here."

He patted the wood slat bottom of the swing. "Come sit with me before I go home. It's a beautiful spring night. Stars and moon and fresh country air."

"You don't want to go home, do you?"

"What?"

"I said, you don't want to go home. You don't want to be alone."

"Smart lady."

"Why didn't you go to Nashville and stay with Tallie

and Peyton instead of coming back to Crooked Oak if you hate being alone?''

"I thought I wanted a quiet, isolated place to hide away," he admitted. "But I've discovered that I'm not a loner. I like contact with other people far too much. Especially certain old friends.''

Sheila laughed. Dear Lord, he was such a flirt. Such a charmer. Those things about Caleb hadn't changed. "Oh, all right, I'll sit in the swing with you for fifteen minutes and then you'll go home and I'll go in to bed.''

"Mmm." He grinned mischievously. "We could skip the fifteen minutes in the swing and forget about my going home and just head straight to your bed.''

She knew he was joking, or at least halfway joking, and wondered how long it had been since he'd laughed and kidded around since the accident.

She sat with him, their side-by-side bodies filling the narrow swing. He slid his arm around her shoulders. She allowed him to touch her, to bring her body close to his, and for a moment she closed her eyes and pretended that there was more than loneliness prompting his actions.

"How long's it been?" he asked, his voice low and husky.

"How long's what been?" she replied.

"Since you got some."

Sheila giggled. "What a question to ask me. You're certainly not a romantic are you, Caleb?''

"Nope. So?"

"'So' what?"

"So, how long has it been since you got some?"

"For your information, I don't get *some*," she said. "I have sex. I make love.''

"Okay. How long's it been since you had sex or made love?''

"Do you think that's any of your business?''

"Maybe not." He slid his left hand beneath her hair and

caressed the nape of her neck. She shuddered. "What if I tell you how long it's been for me? Then will you tell me?"

"Maybe I don't want to know," she said.

"Sure you do." He nuzzled the side of her neck. She shuddered again. "I haven't had sex in a year. Not since before the accident."

His tongue circled her ear. Her mouth formed a surprised oval as she silently gasped. "I—I find that hard to believe. I'm sure there have been dozens of women who—" He kissed her ear at the same moment he speared his fingers into her hair and grasped her head. "Caleb, don't do this to me."

"I could have gotten it on with some of my nurses and even with a willing fan or two who sneaked into my hospital room, but I was in no shape to fool around. And when I recovered enough to go home to my apartment, I went through several months of deep depression."

"I'm sorry. Tallie told me how worried she's been about you."

"Fess up, honey," he said. "I told you, so now it's your turn to tell me. How long's it been?"

"Five years," she said softly.

"Five years!" He grabbed her chin and turned her to face him. "Are you saying you haven't had sex with anyone since your husband died?"

"Yes, that's what I'm saying."

"But why?"

"Because I don't have sex with a man unless he's important to me, unless I care about him and... Don't look at me that way."

"What way?" he asked. "How am I looking at you?"

"Don't." She jumped up from the swing and headed for the front door, but Caleb caught her before her hand reached the knob.

He encircled her body with his arms and pulled her back up against his chest. "You need me as much as I need you.

We could be so good for each other.'' He turned her around and lowered his mouth to hers.

Not only did she want his kiss, she accepted it with enthusiasm, opening her mouth for his invasion. Hot and demanding and all-consuming, his tongue pillaged while his big hand held her head in place and his body pressed intimately against hers. His sex pulsed against her mound, requesting permission for entrance.

She flung her arms around him and held him close, longing to surrender and give him all that he wanted. Every fiber of her being raged with the need for fulfillment. All she had to do was open the door and take him inside the house to her bedroom. And when they were through, he could go home to the farm and no one would ever know what had happened. Just like twelve years ago when they'd made love. The night Danny had been conceived. The night she'd known she would love Caleb Bishop until the day she died.

Breaking the kiss, Sheila breathed deeply, then shoved gently against his chest. If she didn't put a stop to this now, she would live to regret it.

"Go home, Caleb." She laid her hands on his chest. His heart drummed beneath her palm. "I don't want another one-night stand."

Caleb adjusted his aviator sunglasses as he got out of his Porsche. He hadn't actually thought much about stopping by to watch Danny's team this afternoon. In fact, he had decided that maybe Sheila was right—that he shouldn't let the boy become too attached to him. But bored out of his skull, he'd hopped into his car and driven away from the farm. Somehow he'd wound up passing by the grammar school and noticed the boys playing ball. He'd practiced ball out there in Old Man Pickens's field. Some of the happiest days of his life had been spent in Little League.

Rubbing his right arm as he propped his hip against the

hood of the car, he searched the group of boys. It wasn't hard to find Sheila's son. Not only was he a couple inches taller than most of the other guys, the boy's jet-black hair curling out from beneath his ball cap glistened in the late afternoon sunlight.

Caleb kept his distance for quite a while, not wanting his presence to create a scene. He watched the boys and their coach, noticing that Danny seemed to be the chosen pitcher for the team. Caleb's own position. From the first year in Little League until his final year with the Braves. He'd possessed a natural talent that had made him practically a legend by thirty. He had lived for the rush, the unparalleled high, of pitching a great game. But his pitching days were over.

Lifting his useless right arm, he stared at the crippled appendage as if it weren't a part of his own body. A stupid accident. One vital error. A split second and it had all ended. He'd told himself repeatedly that he was luckier than his girlfriend Kimberly, and his teammate Wes Shatz. After all, he had survived the boat wreck. They hadn't.

Caleb watched the practice progress as Coach Lawley stood on the sidelines, instructing the young ballplayers. The man spoke with a soft, authoritative voice. Caleb's gut instincts told him that Pat was the right kind of man to be coaching a bunch of kids. He seemed to be adequately knowledgable about the game, firm in his discipline but still patient and understanding.

At one point, Lawley removed his cap, scratched his head and spit on the ground. He glanced around the parking area, as if searching for something or someone. When he spotted Caleb, he smiled and threw up his hand. Caleb nodded.

As he made his way toward Caleb, Lawley continued making comments to the boys—giving them direction and praise. He came up beside Caleb and offered his hand. The two men exchanged a cordial handshake, then Lawley looked out into the field where *his* boys were playing their hearts out, as if this practice were a title game.

"I appreciate your stopping by, Mr. Bishop. The boys will be thrilled."

"Caleb, not Mr. Bishop."

"Yeah, right. Caleb. I wouldn't mind your giving me a few pointers on how to help these boys. Some of them are good players but a few would be sitting on the bench all the time if they were on someone else's team. I try to give every boy a chance to play during each game."

"Little League needs more coaches with your attitude, Pat," Caleb said. "Those kids will learn soon enough that winning is the name of the game. Too bad they can't just enjoy playing while they're kids. Guess Little League hasn't changed much in all these years, huh?"

"I'm afraid not. Most of these kids are playing for their dads, and too many fathers are trying to relive their childhoods through their sons." Pat shook his head sadly. "And the boys whose fathers don't have the time to coach a team, or be on the board, or who aren't the coach's buddy, are often passed over, whether or not they're good players. I'm afraid the Bulldogs is comprised of boys the other teams didn't want."

"I find that hard to believe." Caleb watched Danny pitch, striking out the batter. "Danny Vance is a damn good pitcher for a boy his age. Are you telling me the other teams didn't want him?"

"Not until recently," Pat said. "Once his mother's best friend became first lady of the state, the other teams were interested, all right. But Sheila and Danny told them no thanks, that if he wasn't good enough for their teams before, he still wasn't."

Caleb snorted. "Dammit! Things are even worse now than back when I played. Believe it or not, I know what it feels like to sit on the bench, to be a kid without a dad coaching or rooting from the sidelines. I didn't get my real chance to be a star pitcher until I played high school baseball.''

"Danny's good. He's a natural, and I give him every opportunity I can to show his stuff.''

"You're fond of him, aren't you?''

"Yeah, I like the kid, and I like Sheila, too. Guess you can say that I've been using the kid to get to his mom.'' Pat grinned shyly.

"Are you and Sheila—?''

"No, we're not, but I'd like for us to be,'' Pat admitted. "We've dated a few times, but she doesn't feel what I do. I never figured she'd be mourning Dan Vance after all these years, but I can't figure out what other reason she'd still be single. Sheila would make some man a good wife.''

"You're right,'' Caleb agreed. "Sheila's the wife and mother type, isn't she?''

"Yeah, she's dependable and loyal and caring. And I've never seen a woman love her child more. She'd do anything for Danny. That's why I can't understand why she hasn't remarried and given him a father.''

"Who knows,'' Caleb replied.

Caleb had wondered why Sheila was still single, why she hadn't found herself a husband and given Danny a father. Had she loved Dan Vance that much? Somehow he couldn't picture Sheila and Dan sharing a passionate love affair. The guy had been twice Sheila's age. Caleb hadn't thought much about it when he'd heard the two had married not long after he'd gone off to college. A few times the thought had crossed his mind that Sheila had married Dan on the rebound. Caleb knew she'd thought she was in love with him after their one night together, and he'd regretted hurting her when he told her that he couldn't return her feelings.

"Take a break, Danny.'' Pat Lawley's strong voice echoed across the field. "We'll let Tanner pitch for a while.''

He turned to Caleb. "Stick around awhile, will you? I need to get back to business, but we'll be finished up here in a few minutes."

Danny came off the field, hiked his glove up under his arm and headed toward a large cooler. He flipped open the lid and retrieved an iced bottle of water. When he took the first sip, he glanced out toward the makeshift parking area and saw Caleb. The boy threw up his hand and waved, then came racing out to meet his idol.

"Hey, Caleb! I knew you'd come. Man, this is great. Come on over and meet the rest of the team. We're about through for the day." Danny grabbed Caleb's right hand and tugged.

Caleb flinched. Instinctively he jerked free from the boy's hold. No one touched his right hand and arm. Most people tried not to even look at it.

"Sorry," Danny said. "That's your injured arm, isn't it?" Without another thought, Danny took Caleb's left hand and led him toward the field.

Caleb slowed his pace, causing Danny to stop and look up at him. "What's the matter?"

"Hadn't we better wait until the guys finish up?"

"I told you that practice is about over," Danny said. "Didn't you notice how many cars have shown up. It's parents and grandparents coming to pick us up."

"Is your mother picking you up today?"

"Yep. We're going to Pete's Café for supper and then we've got to shop for some new jeans for me. These—" he pointed to the pair he wore "—aren't worn out or anything. But see how short they are? Mama says I've got to stop growing sooner or later."

There was something about Danny's smile that affected Caleb in an odd way. Something familiar. Maybe he had Sheila's smile. He certainly had her big, blue eyes. Caleb studied the boy for a minute. No, that wasn't it—Danny's smile wasn't anything like Sheila's.

"Introduce me to your friend, Danny," a syrupy female voice said.

Danny jumped. Caleb jerked his head around. A petite brunette in a pair of skintight jeans smiled at him.

"Oh, hi, there, Mrs. Baker," Danny said. "I didn't hear you come up. This is Caleb Bishop. Caleb, this is Devin's mother."

The brunette held out her small, ring-adorned hand and took a step closer, leaving only inches between her body and Caleb's. "Gwyn Baker, Mr. Bishop. Us folks here in Crooked Oak sure are proud that you're a native son. This whole town watches the Braves religiously. I'm one of your biggest fans myself."

"Thanks."

The minute Caleb accepted the woman's hand, she curled her fingers and clasped tightly. "So, you're Devin's mother, huh? I met him last night at Danny's house."

"I know." Gwyn's full, pouty lips opened in a broad smile. "That's all he talked about when Bill Finch brought him home. He said you might be here today, so I decided to come by and see for myself. Devin usually gets a ride home with one of the other kids."

Caleb extracted his hand from Gwyn's, but couldn't escape her flirtatious smile or her arm that suddenly snaked around his waist.

"Come on, Caleb." Danny tugged on Caleb's arm. "The guys are all dying to meet you."

Completely ignoring Danny, Gwyn said, "If you ever get lonesome or bored, I'd be more than happy to show you around. I know all the hot spots from here to Nashville."

"What would Mr. Baker think about your showing me around?" Caleb asked.

Gwyn's chirpy laughter gained the attention of several other parents who had emerged from the vehicles and were milling around, moving slowly but surely in Caleb's direction.

"There isn't any Mr. Baker, sugar," she said. "Well, there is. But he lives in Arkansas and he's not my husband anymore."

Pat Lawley, followed by the entire Bulldogs team, headed toward Caleb. Surrounded, he thought. Surrounded by fans. There had been a time when he had immensely enjoyed the adoration of the crowds, had loved being swamped by a horde of baseball enthusiasts. But that had been when he was at the top of his game. A star. The idol of millions of boys throughout America. And the heartthrob for a million and one women.

"The team is really glad you stopped by," Pat Lawley said. "How about saying a few words to the boys?"

"Sure thing." Caleb had given plenty of inspirational talks to kids during his reign as the Prince of Baseball. All he had to do was remember one and spiel it off to Danny and his teammates.

After his talk and a half hour spent signing autographs on everything from baseball bats to Gwyn Baker's T-shirt, Caleb realized that despite his disability, he was still the hometown hero. These people were still fans. These boys still worshiped him. And to these women—Gwyn Baker in particular—he was still a heartthrob.

"Have you got plans for dinner tonight?" Gwyn whispered in his ear. "I could get a baby-sitter and we could go over to the Pale Rider for a few beers."

A night with Gwyn Baker might be just what he needed. She seemed to be the type who'd show him a good time and not expect anything else. Just as he started to accept Gwyn's offer, he saw Sheila Vance cross the parking area and head straight toward Danny, who was busy helping Pat Lawley gather up the team's equipment. Pat smiled at Sheila, put his hand on Danny's shoulder and the three of them walked off the field together. They looked like the ideal family.

Caleb's gut tightened. Pat could offer Sheila and her son a commitment, a future as a husband and father. Whereas he couldn't offer them more than a few months of his life, as a lover to Sheila and a buddy to Danny. Pat was the kind of man they needed. He wasn't. He had no right to interfere in Sheila's life, to disrupt anything that might happen between Pat and her.

"I don't have any plans," Caleb told Gwyn. "Tell me where you live and I'll pick you up, say, around seven-thirty."

Gwyn winked at him. "We're going to have us a real good time." She scanned the small group of boys still waiting for rides and called out to her son. "Devin, come on. We've got to go. I'm dropping you by Aunt Brandie's to spend the night."

Gwyn rushed her son to their car and when she backed out, she stuck her head out the window and yelled, "See you at seven-thirty, Caleb. Now don't you be late, sweetie."

Caleb grinned and waved. He felt a hard tug on his left arm and when he looked down, he saw Danny Vance staring up at him.

"Have you got a date with Devin's mom?" he asked.

Sheila and Pat walked up behind Danny. Sheila's gaze locked momentarily with Caleb's.

"Well, yeah, sport, I do. You see—"

"I thought you were going to date Mom and me." Danny swallowed hard. "I know Devin's mom is kind of flashy, but she's not the—"

"Danny, that's enough," Sheila said. "It's not any of your business whom Caleb dates." She gripped her son's tense shoulder.

Danny pulled away from his mother and ran toward their car.

Caleb cleared his throat. "I'm sorry, I—"

"It's all right," Sheila said. "Danny will be okay. It's better he realizes now that there's not going to be anything happening between you and me."

Pat put his arm around Sheila's shoulders. "Why don't I go along with you and Danny over at Pete's tonight?"

Sheila forced a smile. "That sounds like a good idea."

Caleb stood alone in the parking area long after everyone else had left. Why did he feel like a bad guy? Why did it bother him so damn much that he had disappointed Danny Vance? He didn't owe Sheila's son anything and it was best for both him and the boy if they didn't get too tight.

Admit it, Caleb told himself. You like that kid and you want him to like you, to keep on admiring you. You know how it feels to be the only kid on the team whose father is dead. You can relate to Danny, can understand how he feels and what he wants. He wants a father the way you always did.

For some reason Caleb couldn't fathom, a crazy notion crossed his mind. What would it be like to have a son—a boy like Danny? He'd never thought about having children, never considered the possibility that anything was missing from his perfect life. But being back home in Crooked Oak, having spent time with Sheila and her son, made him wonder if something really important hadn't been missing from his life for a long time before the boating accident had ended his career. A wife. Children. A family of his own.

Four

Caleb awoke with a slight hangover, a severe arousal and a rotten attitude. Last night should have been fun. But it hadn't been. He had gone through the motions with Gwyn Baker and it certainly hadn't been her fault that their date had ended so badly. She hadn't been lying when she said she knew all the hot spots between Crooked Oak and Nashville. He thought they'd hit at least half a dozen places, drinking and dancing and partying it up big-time, before he'd brought her back to the farm. Hell, the woman had been all over him, thrilled at the thought of spending the night with the hometown celebrity—the famous Caleb Bishop. Maybe if she'd just kept her mouth shut, if she hadn't gone on and on about him being a superstar, she might still be in his bed this morning.

Or maybe she would be there still if he hadn't been thinking about Sheila Vance the whole time Gwyn had rubbed against him like a cat against her master's leg. Why couldn't he forget the kiss he'd shared with Sheila on her front porch? He had shared more passionate kisses with far more beautiful women. Gwyn to name just one. But when the moment of truth came last night and he had tossed Gwyn down on his bed, he'd looked at the woman lying there, her arms open wide, and he had seen not the sultry petite Gwyn, but Sheila Vance. The momentary apparition had shaken him so badly that he'd made up some stupid excuse and driven his date straight home.

Caleb stumbled into the bathroom, groaned when he saw his bleary-eyed reflection in the mirror, then turned on the faucet and slapped cold water in his face.

You idiot, chided a voice inside his head. *You had a willing woman in your bed last night and you sent her home because of a kiss you shared with Sheila. A kiss. Nothing more. And with Sheila! What's the problem here? Can't your ego take a rejection? Do you want Sheila simply because she said no and you aren't accustomed to being refused?*

Just as Caleb reached out to turn on the shower, the telephone rang. He really didn't want to talk to anyone, but on the off chance it was Tallie checking up on him, he thought he'd better answer, otherwise his baby sister was liable to have the local sheriff out to check on him.

He picked up the receiver. "Yeah?"

"Caleb, this is Mike Hanley. I've found you a 1968 Firebird convertible. It needs a lot of work, but the body's sound. She used to be a beauty and if you're willing to put enough money into her, she can be a showstopper. Are you interested?"

Was he interested? Maybe. The only thing that had ever interested him much, besides baseball and women, was cars, and he'd never forget how much he'd loved his GTO.

At least overseeing the restoration of a car would give him something to occupy his mind until he decided what he was going to do with the next thirty or forty years of his life.

"I'm interested. How soon can you make the deal?"

"The car's here right now, at the garage," Mike said. "All you have to do is come in with your checkbook and you could take possession today."

"Yeah, sure. I'll run by in a while," Caleb said. "How long do you think it'll take to restore her?"

"That depends on how long you want to take." Mike chuckled. "If you're looking to kill some time, we could make the job last for months."

"I haven't tinkered around on a car in a long time, but I think it might do me good to get some grease under my fingernails while I'm killing time."

Sheila pretended not to notice Caleb when he arrived. He was the last person on earth she wanted to see—especially the morning after his big night with Gwyn Baker. She should have known that Gwyn would make a beeline straight to Caleb and that he, being the man he was, would take her up on what she was offering. It wasn't that Sheila disliked Gwyn. Despite the fact that their sons were good friends, she really didn't know Devin's mother all that well. Except by reputation, of course. Everyone in Crooked Oak knew that most men found the pretty, young divorcée irresistible and that people in general considered her irresponsible. Devin spent more time with his aunt than he did his mother. Yeah, Gwyn was just the type of woman Caleb needed—a fun-loving girl who wasn't looking for more than a good time.

"Hey," Caleb called when he entered the garage. "Where's Mike? He's supposed to have an old Firebird waiting here for me."

"Mike took the tow truck out," Sheila said, lifting her gaze from the order form on the desk in front of her. "There was a two-car wreck out on Willow Lane. He'll probably be busy for a couple of hours."

"Anybody hurt?" Caleb asked.

"Nothing serious."

How could one man be so gorgeous? Sheila mused. It just wasn't fair that Caleb was so beautiful and yet at the same time so very masculine. And it certainly wasn't fair that a plain girl like her had fallen head over heels in love with the handsomest man on earth twelve years ago.

"So, should I hang around and wait on Mike, or should I come back later?" Caleb asked, peering over the top of her computer.

"Suit yourself," she replied. "The Firebird is parked out back, so if you'd like to take a look, go right ahead. But if you'd prefer to come back when Mike's here, then you can probably catch Gwyn on her lunch break over at Amber's Beauty Bar."

"Amber's Beauty Bar. Hmm. Yeah, I think she mentioned she'd be free around noon." Caleb noted the slight flush on Sheila's cheeks and wondered if he had mistaken the sharp edge to her voice when she'd mentioned Gwyn. Was it possible that Sheila was jealous?

"I'll tell Mike you'll be by later this afternoon." Returning her attention to the order form she'd been filling out, Sheila dismissed Caleb.

He draped his arms around the computer and leaned over it. Sheila gasped and jumped simultaneously. Caleb grinned mischievously.

"I thought you were going over to Amber's," she said.

"I didn't say I was going anywhere." Caleb rounded the desk and grabbed Sheila's right hand with his left. "I think I'll pass on lunch with Gwyn today."

Sheila jerked her hand out of his grasp and glared at him. "Oh, I see. Gwyn was just another one-night stand for you, huh? She was fun last night, but today you want something different—someone different."

Caleb perched his hip on the edge of Sheila's desk. "I wanted someone different last night, but the lady I really wanted to be with wasn't available."

"Is that right? Who, pray tell, is this unavailable lady you wanted to be with instead of Gwyn Baker? She must really be something, considering Gwyn is the gal every guy in Crooked Oak has the hots for."

"She's something special—my unavailable lady. But the more I pursue her, the more she backs away. Maybe you can help me figure out how to make some points with her."

Sheila raised her gaze quickly, stunned by his request. "I don't have time for your games, Caleb. If you want to play, go play with Gwyn or someone like her."

"You aren't interested in helping me make points with the lady I want?" Caleb asked, a comical forlorn look on his face.

"Will you please go away and leave me alone. All you're doing is trying to aggravate me. I know exactly what you're getting at and it's not going to work. I'm well aware that this unavailable lady you're talking about is me."

"Ah, you guessed my secret." He grabbed her hand, brought it upward and pressed his lips against her soft flesh.

Sheila quivered, the sensation spiraling through her body like a puff of shivering wind. Why was he doing this to her? Why was he pursuing her when there were far more attractive women than she willing to fill his lonely hours? Didn't he realize that she couldn't succumb to his flirtation without losing her heart? And she knew Caleb Bishop. He might actually want her for one night or even several nights. But he wasn't the marrying kind, and that was the only kind of man she needed. She couldn't think only of herself; she had to consider Danny in any decisions she made. Any man she took an interest in would automatically become potential father material in her son's mind. She could hardly have a casual affair with Danny's idol without giving her son false hopes. She might understand that dating Caleb would be only a temporary arrangement, but Danny would delude himself into thinking the new man in his mother's life was going to stick around for the long haul.

She jerked her hand out of his once again. "Tell me something, Caleb—why would you prefer my company to Gwyn Baker's? She's prettier than I am, smaller than I am, more feminine than I am, and I'm sure she's far more experienced in bed than I am."

Caleb was momentarily taken aback. He wasn't accustomed to such frank honesty from a woman. But what had he expected? This wasn't just any woman. This was Sheila Hanley. Sheila Hanley Vance, the only woman, other than his sister, who'd ever been completely straight with him. She hadn't been impressed with his high-school-jock, teen-heartthrob image twelve years ago and she sure as hell wasn't impressed with his superstar-stud image now.

"Who says Gwyn's prettier than you?"

"Don't try that on me!" Narrowing her gaze, she gave him a dirty look. "I'm not some naive teenage girl willing to put out in the back seat just because she thinks the guy she's had a crush on for years has finally fallen for her. That Sheila is long gone, so save your sweet talk for someone gullible enough to believe you."

"I suppose you have a right to still be pissed at me about what happened, but I swear to you, Sheila, I never meant to hurt you."

"So you said, the very next morning. And I believed you. But pardon me if I'm not interested in getting my heart broken a second time by a guy who's just passing through town on his way to the rest of his life."

She shoved back the chair, jumped up and walked away from him, practically running out the side door that led to the fenced area where they parked the junked cars. Why had she brought up the past? Why couldn't she have just played his silly little game, brushed him off and laughed about it later? Good heavens, she'd all but told the man she was still in love with him.

The April noontime sun was warm and bright, heating her skin through her cotton knit shirt and faded jeans. Pressing her forehead to the wooden fence, she closed her eyes and prayed that Caleb had left. She didn't want to face him so soon after her emotional confession.

His big left hand came down on her shoulder, squeezing gently. She trembled from head to toe. Her body tensed at his touch.

"I was an eighteen-year-old kid," he said quietly. "I thought with my pecker and not my head, like most boys that age. I can make all kinds of excuses for why I made love to you that night. Like I'd had too much to drink and I was high on life. I'd just graduated from high school. I had a baseball scholarship. And I was grateful to you for helping me make my dream come true."

"And you had sex with me out of gratitude? Is that what you're trying to say? 'I'll give poor ole, plain Sheila a little thank-you sex and she'll be grateful to me for the rest of her life.'" The anger that had lain dormant in her for twelve years rose to the surface and erupted in a massive outburst. Balling her hands into fists, she turned to face him. "Damn you, Caleb Bishop! You have no idea how much your little thank-you cost me!"

He tightened his hold on her shoulder when she struggled to escape. "It cost you your virginity and I really am sorry about that, especially if it mattered to Dan that there had been somebody before him. And I'm sorry, too, if I broke your heart. I guess I knew, after that night, how you really felt about me, but... I...well, I—"

"But you didn't love me. And you didn't want me. And you had your whole life mapped out. First to make a name for yourself in college baseball and then to go to the major leagues. I didn't figure into your life at all and—and I knew that."

"I guess I didn't realize you still hadn't forgiven me for what happened." Caleb lifted his hand and tenderly caressed her cheek. "I suppose I figured you'd gotten over me a long time ago, that after marrying Dan and having his child, what happened between us wouldn't mean much to you. Was I wrong, Sheila? Did you marry Dan Vance on the rebound? Did he know about me?"

Did Dan know about you, Caleb? Did he know that I loved you? That you'd been my first lover? Of course he knew! How could he not know? I was pregnant with your child when he married me.

Sheila smiled, then laughed. Caleb stepped away and stared at her. She tossed back her head and took a deep breath, all the while chuckling to herself as if amused by some private joke.

"Yes, he knew about you," she said. "Daniel and I didn't have any secrets. He was a good man. A very good man. And he was a wonderful father. He loved Danny more than anything on earth. He had always wanted a child, but he and his first wife didn't have any."

Standing straight and tall, she lifted her chin defiantly. "I haven't spent the past twelve years pining away for you, so don't think that I have. But I haven't forgotten how I felt when you..." She paused and looked directly at him. "When you went away and never came back. Never called. Never wrote. I don't want a repeat performance. I'm not emotionally equipped to handle a brief, meaningless affair today any more than I was equipped to handle a one-night stand twelve years ago."

"You think that's all I'm capable of, don't you? One-night stands and meaningless affairs."

"You tell me," she said. "Do you think you could ever offer a woman more?"

Lowering his head, he looked down at the ground, deliberately breaking eye contact with her. "I honestly don't know." He glanced up and their gazes locked. "But I will tell you this—if you and I have an affair, it won't be meaningless."

"Not to me," she said.

"Nor to me." He turned and walked away, then stopped, glanced over his shoulder and said, "Tell Mike that I'll come back later and take a look at the Firebird."

"I'll tell him."

She watched Caleb disappear around the side of the garage, heard his Porsche start up, and listened as he drove away. Her shoulders slumped, her head drooped and tears gathered in the corners of her eyes. Well, you got what you wanted, didn't you? she told herself. Caleb Bishop isn't going to bother you again. You're safe from making a fool of yourself over him. And Danny's safe from ever finding out the truth.

Pat opened the door of his minivan, took Sheila's arm and assisted her. Settling into the seat after fastening the safety belt, she relaxed and waited for Pat to start the engine. She always enjoyed dates with Pat. He was kind, considerate, and a real gentleman. She supposed if she was a smart woman, she'd allow their relationship to become as serious as he wanted it to be. But as fond as she was of him, she knew that she would never again settle for less than the real thing.

She had been married once to a good man who had treated her well and taken care of her and her son. But she'd never loved Daniel Vance, not the way a woman should love her husband. Her stomach had never fluttered nervously just looking at him. Her body had never sang when he touched her. She had never fallen apart in his arms. Never cried out from the sheer joy of having him inside her. Never held his pillow close after he'd left the bed, simply so she could smell his scent.

She had accepted a marriage without passion once, for Danny's sake. But she would never do it again. Not for any reason. If she ever married again, it would be for love and love alone.

"Did you enjoy the movie?" Pat asked as he started the van.

"Oh, yes, I like romantic comedies. I hope you weren't bored. Danny would have hated it. He is such a typical male."

"Well, I guess it's a good thing Bill Finch took the boys bowling tonight."

"Bill's kind enough to include Danny in a lot of his activities with Tanner. He realizes how difficult it is for Danny not to have a father."

Pat looked at her before setting the van into gear.

"Sheila, you know how much I care about Danny and about—"

"Pat, I thought we agreed that tonight's date would be just fun. No serious discussions."

"Sorry," he said. "You're right. Just fun tonight." He slowed the van and nodded toward the brightly lit building on the left of the road. "What do you say we stop by the Pale Rider? We could have a drink and dance a little? I know it's not the kind of place you'd ordinarily go to, but I just thought since—"

"I'd love to go to the Pale Rider for a drink. And I haven't danced since Mike's wedding."

They entered the smoky interior of Crooked Oak's one and only nightspot, a good ole boy's paradise of country music, cheap beer and women on the make. Sheila had been inside the roadhouse only once before, and she'd never forget that night. It was the night Tallie Bishop had gotten in the middle of a fistfight between Eric Miller and Peyton Rand. Tallie had wound up breaking Eric's nose. And that was the same night her other best friend, Susan Williams, had danced with Lowell Redman, her future husband, for the first time.

"Do you see an empty table?" Pat asked, peering through the smoke.

"There's one." Sheila pointed out a table to the right,

near the back of the crowded room. But just as they headed for the empty spot, another couple took occupancy. "Oh, well." Sheila shrugged her shoulders.

"Would you like to dance first?" Pat suggested. "Then if we can't find a table, we can have a beer at the bar."

"Fine with me." She practically shouted her reply because the band had just struck up a new foot-patting beat.

Standing as tall as he at five foot ten, Sheila went into Pat's arms and smiled directly at him. They moved to the rhythm of the upbeat music, the zing of a steel guitar buzzing in their ears.

God, it was good to relax and have a good time. Good not to worry about life's daily chores. Good not to have to think about a man who held the power to destroy the tranquility of her life.

Smiling contentedly as Pat whirled her around the dance floor, Sheila caught a glimpse of another couple next to them and for one brief moment her heart stopped. She should have known better than to come into the Pale Rider on a Friday night. She should have known that Caleb Bishop would be here with another woman. Gwyn Baker had her arms draped around Caleb's neck and her body pressed intimately against his. Her head rested on his chest and Caleb's left hand cupped her hip. A sick feeling hit Sheila square in the stomach.

Don't do this to yourself. You sent him away. You told him that you didn't want him on his terms. He has every right to go to another woman for what you aren't willing to give him.

"Well, hi, there, you two," Gwyn said. "Look, Caleb, it's Sheila and Pat. Shoot fire, I never thought I'd see you in here, Sheila."

"We just stopped by for a drink, but decided to go ahead and dance since we couldn't find a table," Pat explained.

"Hey, why don't y'all share our table? We've got room." She grabbed Caleb's left hand, then reached out and grabbed Pat's arm. "Come on. We'll order a fresh round of drinks and talk for a while."

Sheila and Caleb exchanged a quick, uncertain glance, before Sheila reluctantly followed Pat's lead and joined the couple at their nearby table.

"So, you two are dating again, huh?" Gwyn leaned over and wrapped her arm around Caleb's neck. "You probably don't know this," she told Caleb, "but Pat's been trying to get to first base with Sheila for nearly two years now and she keeps playing hard to get."

Sheila realized that Gwyn Baker was, as the old folks said, "three sheets to the wind." Wondering if Pat felt as uncomfortable as she did, she glanced his way and noted the pink flush creeping up his neck and spotting his cheeks.

Ignoring Gwyn's tactless comment, Caleb ordered a round of drinks and tried to dislodge her tenacious hold from around his neck.

"I say you're a fool not to take Pat up on what he's got to offer," Gwyn advised. "After all, it's not easy finding a man interested in marrying women like us, who aren't so young anymore and are saddled with kids. And it's got to be even harder for you, honey, considering you don't exactly come equipped with all the stuff men seem to like so much. You know—a pretty face, a skinny body and big boobs."

"Would you mind if I dance with your date?" Caleb asked Pat as he eased back his chair and offered Sheila his hand.

"No, er, not at all," Pat said, obviously uncertain how to respond to Gwyn's blatant insult or Caleb's unexpected request.

Sheila hesitated momentarily, then decided it would be simpler and easier to accept Caleb's offer than to sit awkwardly at the table and try to be pleasant after Gwyn's unintentionally rude comment.

Caleb didn't say a word as he led her through the crowd

and onto the dance floor. She understood that he was simply trying to diffuse a potentially explosive situation, but she wished he'd found another way. Something that didn't require him taking her into his arms.

She closed her eyes as the pain spread through her mind and body. She didn't want his pity. Couldn't bear for him to feel sorry for her. She didn't need any more crumbs of kindness from him.

It would be so easy to relax in his arms, to allow the intimate sway of their bodies moving in unison to overrule her common sense. But she didn't dare give in to her deepest, heartfelt yearnings. She'd done that once and lived to regret her foolishness.

He caressed her back with gentle, circular motions, his actions soothing the tension boiling inside her. As he pulled her closer, he lowered his head and whispered in her ear, "She was wrong, you know."

Don't, she wanted to scream. *Don't say anything stupid. Don't try to make things right.* "She wasn't wrong. I've always known my shortcomings as a woman. I've just never had anyone point them out so frankly."

"Gwyn's drunk," he said. "She has no idea she said anything inappropriate."

"I know she's had too much to drink and I know she didn't mean to be unkind," Sheila said just as the band finished their tune. She moved out of Caleb's arms and turned, but before she could take one step, he grabbed her wrist and pulled her back into his embrace.

"Gwyn was wrong about your not being pretty," Caleb said. "You are pretty."

"You're just making matters worse by lying to me," she told him. "I've known all my life that I was a big, rawboned girl. Lord knows, I've never been skinny. I don't have large breasts and I'm as plain as an old shoe."

"I'm not lying. I do think you're pretty. You have a fresh, wholesome beauty." While his right arm draped her waist, he eased his left hand up and under her chin-length hair. Grasping her neck, he urged her face closer to his.

She sucked in a deep, nervous breath and gazed into his dark eyes. "Are you trying to sweet-talk me, Caleb Bishop?"

"Yes, ma'am, I am." He pressed his cheek against hers and held her body intimately to his.

Sighing, she closed her eyes and decided to enjoy the moment, fleeting as it was. One perfect moment wrapped in Caleb's arms. Maybe it wouldn't hurt to pretend, for just a little while, that she was pretty and he really did want her, that perhaps he loved her just a little bit.

She gasped softly when she felt his arousal. Her eyes flew open and she stared at him in surprise. He grinned at her.

"I'm attracted to big, rawboned girls who fill my arms completely and gaze longingly at me with their pretty blue eyes and shiver when I touch them." He led her in a slow, sensual dance across the room, then pulled her into a darkened corner hallway near the rear exit.

"Caleb, what do you think you're doing?" she asked when he pushed her up against the wall and braced his left hand beside her head.

He leaned into her, his lips almost touching hers. "You're pretty and sweet and smart, and I like you a lot, Sheila Hanley."

Her mouth gaped open. Her eyes rounded wide and full. "That—that's exactly what you said that night. The night...graduation night...in your car."

"I know. I remember. And I meant every word I said to you that night. You *were* pretty and sweet and smart, and I did like you a lot. I never—ever—meant to hurt you. It's just that you were such a damn powerful temptation that I couldn't resist taking you. Having a smart, sweet girl like you care about a dumb jock like me kind of went to my head. I wanted you so much that night."

"But you didn't love me. Guys like you don't fall in love with girls like me." She tried to escape from him, but he shoved his body into hers, pinning her against the wall.

"From my experience, love is highly overrated. I've thought I was in love several times and it didn't amount to anything. It didn't last. But liking a woman—I mean genuinely liking her—is a rare thing for me. Except for Tallie, you're the only female I've ever really liked."

"You like me?"

"I like you a whole heck of a lot."

"You date women like Gwyn. You adore them, make love to them, but you don't like them."

"I've never made love to another woman I liked, a woman who was my friend before she became my lover. You're the only one."

When he nuzzled her neck, she closed her eyes and melted against him. "Caleb, I can't handle this. You just want me because I'm a challenge, because I keep turning you down. You're bored and need some kind of diversion to take your mind off your troubles."

The kiss came so quickly that she had no time to protest. His lips covered hers with breath-robbing intensity. His sex throbbed against her belly. His tongue delved deeply into the moist cavern of her mouth. And she was lost to the power of his passion.

"Excuse me." A man bumped into Caleb's back as he passed them in the dark hallway. "Don't let me disturb you two. I'm just slipping out the back way."

Caleb ended the kiss abruptly. Breathing erratically, Sheila shoved him away and ran down the hallway and into the crowded, noisy throng. She quickly made her way back to the table where Gwyn was entertaining Pat with an off-color joke.

"Where's Caleb?" Gwyn asked.

"He'll be back in a minute," Sheila replied. "I think he went to the rest room." She turned to Pat. "I'm sorry to be a party pooper, but I have a splitting headache. Would you mind taking me home?"

"No, of course I don't mind," Pat said. "Do you need to stop by the drugstore and pick up some medicine or anything?"

"No, I'll take some aspirin when I get home and go straight to bed."

"Now that sounds like a good idea to me," Gwyn said just as Caleb joined them. "Pat, you take Sheila straight home to bed." Gwyn giggled. "And I'll take our home-town superstar home to bed with me."

"Good night." Sheila didn't even glance at Caleb when she took Pat's arm and walked away with him.

Caleb watched until they exited the building, then looked at Gwyn, who had apparently drank another beer while he'd danced with Sheila. He jerked back her chair and lifted her to her feet.

"Come on. I'll take you home while you can still stand."

She wrapped herself around him. "Looks like everybody's gonna have fun tonight."

An hour later Caleb drove by Sheila's house. He couldn't believe he was actually doing this—checking to see if Pat Lawley's minivan was parked in the drive. The small, neat clapboard house was dark and quiet. And the only vehicle in the drive was Sheila's Jeep.

He let out a deep breath, suddenly realizing how much it mattered to him that Sheila hadn't let Pat stay the night.

He'd like to knock on the door, wake her up and tell her that he hadn't taken Gwyn up on her offer, that he'd left a mighty unhappy woman screaming obscenities at him from her front porch. He wasn't going to see Gwyn Baker again. Dating her even once had been a mistake. There was only one woman in Crooked Oak he wanted. One woman who could appease the ache inside him. One woman he needed in his bed.

And that woman had no idea of the power she held over him.

Five

"**M**y goodness, what's all the commotion about?" Susan Redman turned around in the bleachers and craned her neck to look over the crowd that had formed near the entrance to the Little League park.

"I have no idea," Sheila said. "But you'd think the president had arrived."

"It wouldn't be Peyton, would it? I just talked to Tallie yesterday and she didn't mention anything about them making a trip home this weekend."

"Guess I'd better go check it out." Sheriff Lowell Redman rose from his padded stadium seat and made his way down the bleachers, being careful not to step on anyone. By the time he headed toward the mob scene at the ballpark entrance, a man burst through the horde that was following close on his heels.

"Hey, it's Caleb!" Lowell called out to his wife and Sheila. "That's even better than a visit from the president or the governor."

"I should have known," Sheila mumbled.

"What's wrong with you?" Susan asked, then glanced around at the people sitting nearby. Leaning closer, she whispered in Sheila's ear, "Are you worried about Caleb staying in Crooked Oak long enough to start wondering about Danny?"

Sheila glared at her friend and snapped, "Will you hush! Someone's liable to hear you."

"Gossip being what it is in this town, I think you should know that Gwyn Baker's—"

"I know he's been seeing her!"

"Don't bite my head off," Susan said. "They've had two dates, but Gwyn couldn't seduce him, if you know what I mean."

"Susan, how on earth would you know something like that?"

"Seems Gwyn's been sharing tidbits of her love life with the customers over at Amber's. Kay Struthers told Becky McKinney, who told me, that Gwyn thinks there's another woman in Caleb's life. Some woman right here in Crooked Oak." Susan paused for effect, then smiled and asked coyly, "Got any idea who this other woman might be?"

"You shouldn't listen to gossip."

"Probably not, but when it's about Caleb Bishop and one of my best friends, then I listen."

Sheila glanced around at the parents, friends and other Little League supporters surrounding them. "Well, if you keep talking, some of these people are going to be listening to every word you say."

"Look, here comes Lowell," Susan said. "And he's bringing Caleb with him."

Sheila cringed. Caleb was coming straight toward her, making his way upward, through the crowd of friendly, curious townspeople, who kept delaying him to say hello, to shake his hand, to offer him a warm welcome home.

Lowell sat beside his wife, who scooted over to make

room between her and Sheila. "I told Caleb that the next time he decides to show up at a game, he might want to call me first so I can arrange for one of my deputies to act as a bodyguard." Lowell chuckled.

"Hello, Caleb. It's good to see you," Susan said. "What do you think of our new Little League field?"

"It's a great improvement over the one where we played as boys, huh, Lowell?" Caleb sat between the two women, then turned to the one on his left. "How are you tonight, Sheila?"

Forcing a smile, she replied. "Fine, thank you."

"What prompted you to come out to a Little League game?" Lowell asked. "Susan and I try to catch as many of Danny's games as possible. You know Susan is Danny's godmother."

"I came to the game for the same reason y'all did," Caleb said. "I came to see Danny play."

Sheila bit down on her bottom lip and prayed Susan would keep her mouth shut. Other than Mike, Susan was the only person on earth who knew Daniel Vance wasn't Danny's real father.

"So, Danny got to you," Susan said. "I'll bet he invited you and you couldn't resist watching a young pitcher who probably reminds you of yourself at that age."

Sheila's stomach knotted painfully. A tense ache spread across her head. She wanted to tell Susan to shut up, to leave well enough alone, but protesting would only worsen the matter.

"Yeah, I suppose you're right," Caleb said. "I watched him at practice the other day and he's good. Maybe better than I was at his age."

"I told Sheila she should have let him move to another team, that Pat's Bulldogs haven't ever won a championship," Lowell said. "But she and Danny are loyal to the team he's played on since his first year."

"I think Sheila did the right thing. She's obviously

taught Danny what's really important in life.'' When Caleb laid his hand over Sheila's where it rested on the bleacher seat between them, he looked directly at her. ''I'm just beginning to learn that valuable lesson.''

Sheila didn't remove her hand nor look away. Instead she smiled at him, foolishly touched by his compliment and too easily seduced by the look in his dark eyes.

As the ball game progressed, Caleb became aware of some mistakes Pat was allowing the boys to make—mistakes that probably would cost them the game, despite Danny's brilliant pitching. The more he watched Sheila's son, the more amazed he was at the boy's natural talent. And there was something else, some odd, nagging little feeling in the pit of his stomach. Watching Danny was like turning back the clock and observing himself as a kid. Tall, skinny, perfectly coordinated. Passionate about the game. Blessed with a God-given ability far superior to the average player.

A twinge of regret, a fleeting moment of sadness and the realization that he'd missed out on something truly important, moved through him. Fatherhood. *But it's not too late,* a voice inside him said. *You're only thirty. You've got plenty of time.* But he wasn't worried about running out of time. What concerned him was finding the right woman to be the mother of his child. His track record with the fairer sex wasn't exactly great. Most of his relationships didn't last longer than a year, if that. When the time came, what he needed was a special lady. Someone like Sheila Vance.

He shook his head. Hell! Where had that notion come from anyway? He wasn't the marrying kind and didn't intend to be for many years. Maybe never. It wasn't like him to get sentimental over some kid, even a boy who reminded him of himself.

''Hey, Caleb, you ought to go down there and give Pat a few pointers,'' Lowell suggested. ''Our team needs some help or we're going to lose this game.''

"Pat might not appreciate any unsolicited advice," Caleb said.

"Heck, not Pat. He'd welcome your advice," Lowell said. "As a matter of fact, I've seen him looking up here in the stands directly at you a couple of times. I think he'd like for you to help coach from the sidelines."

"Go ahead, Caleb." Susan poked him with her elbow. "Danny can't win this game all by himself."

"What do you think?" Caleb asked Sheila.

"If you want to help Danny's team, then go down there and give Pat all the advice you can. He's a dear, sweet man, but that doesn't necessarily make him a great coach."

The Bulldogs won the game by a run, a homer hit by Danny Vance. The Bulldog supporters went wild, so unaccustomed to winning a game, especially against the Eagles, whose coach would stoop to any level to win. In the after-game frenzy, Caleb put his arm around Sheila and kept her at his side, while grateful parents made their way over to thank the former major league player. And everyone, including the Eagles' supporters, ignored the childish reaction of the losing team's coach.

Danny ran straight to Caleb, who instinctively reached out for the boy, giving him a congratulatory, manly hug around the shoulders.

"Wow, what a game." Danny beamed with the joy of victory. "I've never been so happy in my life."

"We can thank Caleb for helping us win that game." Pat Lawley, with one hand on Tanner Finch's shoulder and the other on Devin Baker's back, grinned from ear to ear. "Great game, guys. I knew you had it in you."

"You boys played your hearts out," Caleb said. "This is your night. How about a pizza party on me?"

The boys cheered wildly. The parents agreed that the whole team would meet up at Martino's Pizza Parlor on

Main Street for a victory celebration, courtesy of the hometown baseball legend.

"Can I ride with Caleb?" Danny asked. "Please, Mom. Please."

Caleb, his arm still draped around Danny's shoulder, said, "Yes, Mom, please."

"Okay. You go with Caleb. I'll get Susan and Lowell to drop me by Martino's."

"You didn't bring your Jeep?" Caleb asked.

"Nah, we rode with Susan and Lowell," Danny said.

"Then why don't we let your mom come along with us and save the Redmans a trip."

"Yeah, Mom. Great idea. Ride with Caleb and me."

"We'll be awfully crowded in Caleb's Porsche," Sheila said.

"It doesn't matter, Mom. I'll scrunch up and make room. Come on. Ride with us. Please."

She had no choice and she knew it. And so did Caleb. He grinned at her with the same cocky, mischievous grin that had haunted her dreams for twelve years.

The Bulldogs and their parents took over the pizza parlor that night and celebrated in high fashion like the victors they were. Gwyn Baker, who had shown up fifteen minutes before the game ended, spent the entire party watching Caleb. The other woman's perusal extended to Sheila every time Caleb looked at Sheila, smiled at her or touched her, which he did often. And Gwyn's close scrutiny made Sheila uncomfortable since the woman's obvious jealousy was apparent to everyone there.

"If looks could kill, you'd be dead right now," Teresa Finch whispered to Sheila. "Gwyn isn't used to being dumped, so she's probably out for blood. She doesn't like the attention Caleb is giving you. And I'll bet she's trying to figure out why Caleb prefers you to her."

A light blush covered Sheila's cheeks. Dear Lord, was it

that apparent that Caleb Bishop was all but courting her right there in front of dozens of her friends and neighbors? There was no telling what people would be saying about her and Caleb come morning. And that's exactly what she didn't want to happen. She didn't want the townspeople connecting her to Caleb Bishop in a romantic way. One thing might lead to another and someone was bound to notice that Danny resembled Caleb, had his natural athletic abilities, and had been born about nine months after Caleb left town twelve years ago.

She had lived with the lie that Daniel Vance was Danny's father for those twelve years, had taught that lie to her son and had fooled the good people of Crooked Oak. And she had been comfortable with that lie, until Caleb's homecoming. She had thought that he and Danny would never meet and she'd been certain that Caleb would never become a part of her life again. She'd been wrong on both counts.

If Caleb meant to stay in Crooked Oak, if he was the kind of man who wanted to settle down and have a family, she might risk telling him the truth and facing the town's scorn and Danny's shock, perhaps even his anger and hatred. But she couldn't—wouldn't—risk everything for a casual affair with a man who could offer her and her son nothing but heartache.

Caleb draped his left arm around Sheila's shoulder and tugged her up against his side. ''What are you two whispering about over here in the corner?

''About hell's fury,'' Teresa said, her smile deepening the dimples in her round, full face.

''What?'' Caleb stared at her quizzically.

''Inside joke,'' Sheila explained.

''Women stuff, huh,'' he said.

''What's this about women stuff?'' Bill Finch asked jokingly as he slipped his arm around his wife's waist.

''Don't tell me that our star pitcher's and our star shortstop's mothers are tired of talking baseball and are actually discussing hairstyles and hem lengths and Mel Gibson," Pat Lawley said when he joined the foursome.

"Well, our little private conversation certainly got out of hand quickly, didn't it?" Teresa smiled at Sheila, then patted her husband on the butt and said, "Come on. Let's get our son and go home. It's nearly eleven o'clock and we have church in the morning."

Bill Finch offered his calloused construction worker's hand to Caleb, who accepted it in a cordial shake. "Thanks for picking up the tab for this shindig. The boys will remember this night as long as they live. A winning ball game and a pizza party afterward, hosted by *the* Caleb Bishop."

"Honest truth, Bill, I think I had more fun than the boys," Caleb said, tightening his hold around Sheila's shoulders.

"Well," Pat confessed, "I've got to thank you again for the advice you gave us. Guess I was just too close to the forest to see the trees."

"Moving Kyle from second base to the outfield really took advantage of his strong throwing arm. And telling the boys to *coil* when the pitcher goes into his windup allowed them to adjust to the different pitches."

One by one, all the fathers thanked Caleb and all the mothers gushed over him just a little. All except Gwyn Baker, who left early with Devin.

"Well, let's head for home, you two." Caleb noticed Danny yawning. He reached over and knocked the boy's cap sideways.

"Hey, I'm awake." Danny laughed. "Could you stay awhile after you take us home? I don't want this night to ever end."

Neither do I, Caleb thought. *There's nothing I'd like better than to stay awhile at your house after I take y'all home. I'd like to help your mom tuck you in and see you look up*

*at me with adoration in your eyes when you say good-night.
And I'd like for your mother to invite me to spend the night
in her bed.*

"That's up to your mother," Caleb said.

"Can he, Mom? Please?"

"For a few minutes," Sheila agreed.

When Danny went to sleep leaning against his mother in
the bucket seat of Caleb's Porsche, Caleb thought about
how inconvenient a sports car was for a family man. Then
he reminded himself that he wasn't a family man, just a
lonely guy playing Dad for one night. If a year ago someone had told him that he'd be living back in his hometown,
courting a widow with a kid and wishing that kid was his,
he'd have laughed in that person's face. Hell, he hadn't
given Sheila Hanley—Sheila Hanley *Vance*—more than a
passing thought in twelve years. And the last thing he'd
wanted was a child. A family wouldn't have fit into his
life-style before the accident. *And it still doesn't,* he told
himself.

When Caleb pulled the Porsche up into the Vance driveway, Sheila shook her son gently. "Wake up, sleepyhead."

"Huh?" Danny's eyelids fluttered, but he didn't open
his eyes.

"I could carry him, if it wasn't for this bad arm," Caleb
said as he opened the driver's door.

"He can walk." Sheila grabbed Danny's chin and softly
shook his face. "Come on, Mr. Baseball. We're home."

"Okay." He yawned, opened his eyes and smiled sleep-
ily at his mother. "Caleb's a great guy, isn't he? Sure wish
he was my dad."

Sheila glanced at Caleb, who had just opened the passenger door, and her heart caught in her throat. *Oh, dear
God, why did you let this happen? Everything was just fine
until Caleb came back into our lives.*

Suppressing her chaotic thoughts, she eased out of the

car, then tugged on Danny's hands until he crawled out behind her. He slid his long, skinny arm around his mother's waist and then reached out and took Caleb's left hand. When the three of them reached the front door, Sheila unlocked it, reached inside to flip on the overhead light in the living room and gently guided Danny inside before turning to Caleb.

"Thanks for the ride home," she said.

"I thought I'd been invited in to stay for a while."

"That was when Danny was still awake. He's asleep on his feet. I'll do good to get him out of his clothes before he passes out."

"Let me come in and put him to bed," Caleb suggested. "You could fix us something to drink—maybe some decaf coffee or—"

"Why don't you just go on home, Caleb?"

"Ah, Mom, let him come in and put me to bed," Danny said.

They turned around and looked at the boy standing just inside the living room. His eyes were half-closed and he was yawning, but his lips were curved into a silly smile.

"Oh, all right," Sheila said. "Help Danny to bed and I'll fix us some coffee." She checked her watch. "It's eleven-thirty. You can stay until midnight."

Sheila went into the house and Caleb followed her, then closed and locked the door behind them. "What happens then?" he asked teasingly. "Do I turn back into a pumpkin or do you lose a glass slipper or—"

"Neither. At midnight you leave and I go to bed."

Caleb grinned, that naughty, irresistible grin that their son had inherited from him. "Okay. I'll leave at midnight, if I have to."

"You have to."

"Come on, sport, let's get you to bed." Caleb followed the sleepy child down the hall to his room—a room filled with baseball paraphernalia. Baseball posters filled the walls, mostly posters of Atlanta Braves' star pitcher, Caleb Bishop.

Danny slumped down on his bed. "Gosh, Caleb, I'm sorry I'm so sleepy. I can't seem to keep my eyes open. I wanted us to talk about the game."

"We can do that later. Right now, you need your rest. You played a great game and wore yourself out. Pitching an entire game the way you did is rough on a guy."

"I did good, didn't I?"

"You did better than good," Caleb told him. "You were a real star tonight."

"Just like you." Danny yawned.

Caleb sat beside Danny on the bed and pulled the child's Bulldogs jersey over his head. "Yeah. Just like me."

Caleb had the strangest urge to reach out and take Sheila's son into his arms. He felt the boy's desperate need to connect to a father figure, to a man he liked and admired. The crazy thing was, he liked the idea of being Danny's father. There was something about this kid—something that got to him.

Just like his mother, Caleb thought. What was it about Sheila that got under his skin, that made him want her to the exclusion of any other woman in Crooked Oak? Sheila was hardly his type. She'd never been his type. But he liked her. He respected her. She was the most honest person he'd ever known. No pretense. No falsehoods. No lies. She was exactly what she seemed. A good woman.

Caleb helped Danny finish undressing, then he pulled the covers down and Danny slipped beneath them. When he gazed up at Caleb with drooping eyelids, Caleb patted him on his cheek. "I'll see you tomorrow. We'll toss the ball around together."

"Promise?"

"Yeah. As long as it's all right with your mother."

Caleb turned off the light, closed the bedroom door and went down the hall toward the kitchen. He found Sheila sitting at the round oak table, a cup of freshly brewed coffee in her hand. When he entered the room, she glanced up and nodded toward the cup sitting on a coaster in front of the chair across from her.

"He went out like a light," Caleb said. "He was worn-out."

"This was a perfect night for Danny, you know." Holding the cup in both hands, she lifted it to her lips.

"It was a pretty good night for me, too. I haven't felt this alive since... Well, not in a long time."

"Sit down, Caleb. We need to talk."

He sat, lifted the cup and sipped the coffee.

"Caleb, I'm grateful for everything you did for the Bulldogs tonight and for helping give Danny an experience he'll never forget, but... I don't know how to say this."

"Just say it."

She set her cup down on the coaster, took a deep breath, laid her hands flat on the tabletop and leaned toward him. "Danny's becoming too fond of you. Before you came to Crooked Oak, you were an idol he worshiped from afar. Now you're a man he admires—up close and personal. And...well, tonight he—he—"

"He said he wished I was his dad, and you think that's a bad thing for him."

"No. Yes. Oh, shoot! It's bad because he's getting too fond of you and he's already wishing you were his dad. And despite what you say to him, or I say to him, if you continue being a part of his life, it's going to kill him when you leave town for good. He's not going to understand how you could walk away and not look back."

"Are we talking about the present, about Danny?" Caleb asked.

"What do you mean? Of course, we're talking about—Oh, I see." Sheila shoved back her chair and stood. Clenching her hands tightly, she glared at Caleb. "You think I'm talking about myself. About twelve years ago when you walked away from me and never looked back.''

''Is that what we're talking about?''

''I don't know. Maybe. Yes, partly,'' she admitted as she slammed her fist down on the table. ''Dammit, Caleb. I will not let you hurt my son the way you hurt me. I won't let you play father to him for a few months while you're passing time here in Crooked Oak. I won't let you make him love you and then see his heart broken when you don't have a place in your life for him anymore.''

''Whoa! Wait just a minute.'' Caleb set down his cup, stood and rounded the table, halting directly in front of Sheila. ''Where is all this anger coming from, honey?''

Oh, God, she'd done it now. The very thing she'd wanted to avoid. She had made Caleb suspicious. She could hardly tell him the truth. *The anger is coming from the fact that you got me pregnant and never once considered the consequences of our one night together.* She couldn't say, *I married a good, kind man old enough to be my father because I didn't want your son to be labeled a bastard.*

Grabbing her chin, Caleb forced her to face him. ''Do you really hate me?''

Clamping her mouth shut tightly, she shook her head. Oh, God, if only she could hate him!

He gazed deeply into her eyes and asked again, ''Do you hate me?''

''No.'' The one word rushed from her lips after an indrawn breath.

Loosening his grip on her chin, he cupped her face in his left hand, then rubbed his thumb across her bottom lip. She sighed, unable to stop herself from responding.

''I don't know what it is about you,'' he said, his voice low and soft and husky. ''In all honesty—and I want to be honest with you, Sheila—I haven't given you much thought over the years. But ever since that first night I came back to town and found you at the farmhouse, I haven't been able to get you off my mind.''

"I can't imagine why.'' Her insides quivered uncontrollably and she prayed she wouldn't start shaking externally, too. "I'm hardly the unforgettable type, am I?''

"If that's true, why do I seem to have you on my mind, night and day? I could have had Gwyn and probably a dozen more women in Crooked Oak, but I don't want Gwyn or anyone else. I want you.''

"You want me only because I keep saying no.'' She laid her hand over his and pulled it away from her face. He threaded their fingers together. "I said yes to you once. Remember? You've had me. I'm already a notch on Caleb Bishop's bedpost.''

"You were never that, honey. If you don't believe anything else, believe that.''

"Then what was I, Caleb? A charity case?''

"Dammit, woman!'' He grabbed her by the back of the neck and jerked her up against him. His lips swooped down and took hers in a hard, hot, ravaging kiss.

She trembled as desire sprung to life inside her, rippled over her nerve endings and set her belly on fire. Then, unexpectedly, he ended the kiss and shoved her away from him.

"Have you ever thought that maybe I'm not the same selfish kid who took you in the back seat of my car? Have you even once considered the fact that back then I might not have been mature enough to appreciate what a very special girl you were, and that now I'm man enough to recognize and to want a real woman when she comes into my life?''

She stood there, her mouth gaping open, her eyes wide as saucers, and watched him turn around and walk out of the kitchen. By the time she could make her legs move, she heard the front door slam.

"Caleb!''

She rushed after him, through the living room and out onto the front porch. He was just about to get into his Porsche when she called out his name again. He turned and looked back at her.

"I don't hate you. I never have."

"Could we start over again?" he asked. "Wipe the slate clean? If I asked you for a date, would you go out with me?"

"I—I might," she said. "Why don't you call and ask me sometime?"

"I just might do that." He got in his car and drove away.

Sheila hugged herself, there on her front porch, with the cool spring breeze chilling her as the mantel clock in the living room struck midnight.

Six

"The whole thing was Mayor Frost's idea," Susan said. "Then the city council got behind it and now they're giving a big bash at the country club next Saturday night to honor Crooked Oak's one and only superstar—Caleb Bishop."

"I wonder how Caleb feels about the party." Sheila retrieved the can from the cola machine outside the garage, handed it to Susan and then inserted more quarters. "He certainly seems to have changed his mind about being left alone."

Susan popped the lid on the soft drink. "Lowell said Caleb agreed to attend, even promised he'd bring a date." Susan took several sips of the syrupy liquid, then gazed inquiringly at Sheila. "He hasn't called and asked you, has he?"

"No, of course not. Why should he?" Sheila lifted a grape soda from the machine, opened it and brought it to her mouth. She wouldn't admit, not even to one of her dearest friends, that she'd been waiting more than a week for Caleb to call and ask her out. She'd been so sure he'd call.

"Well, the local busybodies say he hasn't seen Gwyn again and the odds are that you're the woman in his life now."

"Damn busybodies! I knew this would happen if Caleb showed the least interest in me and Danny. People will start putting two and two together and figure out—"

"Calm down," Susan said. "No one is going to figure out that Caleb is really Danny's father. Not a soul in this town knew that you and Caleb were ever anything more than friends. Even Tallie never suspected the truth. How you hid your feelings from her all these years, I'll never know."

"I hope you're right, because I have no idea how I'd deal with things if Caleb and Danny ever found out that I'd lied to both of them all these years." Sheila walked back inside the garage, swung open the door to her air-conditioned office and waited for Susan to catch up with her.

Sheila sat in the swivel chair at her desk, while Susan unpacked their hamburgers and fries and spread them out on paper napkins.

"If you'd gotten serious about Pat Lawley last year when y'all were dating on a regular basis, the two of you would be married now and you wouldn't be faced with the problem of how to deal with Caleb." Susan pulled a straight-back wooden chair up to the desk. "I know Pat doesn't exactly make you go weak in the knees, but he'd be a good husband and a good father."

"I've already been married to a man who was a good husband and a good father," Sheila said. "If I ever marry again, it will be because I'm so madly in love I can't see straight."

"Aren't you being foolish to think Caleb Bishop is your Prince Charming?" Susan sat in the chair. "Look, I know exactly how you felt about him when we were in high school. You had as big a crush on Caleb as I did on his brother Hank. The only difference was that Hank never thought of me as anything but his kid sister's little friend. You've been pining away all these years for something that's never going to happen. What if I'd waited around hoping Hank Bishop would return to Crooked Oak and sweep me off my feet? Well, I'll tell you what—I'd be thirty-two and still single. Lowell Redman might not give me butterflies in my stomach, but I love him dearly and we're very happy together.''

"There's one slight difference in your situation and mine,'' Sheila said. "You and Hank never had sex and you never gave birth to his child.''

"No, you're right. Hank never even kissed me.''

"Stop worrying about me. Just because I don't intend to settle for what I can get doesn't mean I'm going to succumb to Caleb Bishop's boyish charm and let him ruin my life.''

"I talked to Tallie and she's probably going to call you.'' Susan lifted her hamburger to her mouth.

"What did you tell Tallie? Did you mention that folks around here are speculating about Caleb and me being a couple?''

Susan chewed the bite, swallowed it and then gulped down some cola. "Tallie doesn't agree with me. But then, she doesn't know everything I know. She thinks you're just what the doctor ordered for Caleb. Don't be surprised if she tries to talk you into dating him.''

"Maybe I should date him.''

"What?''

"Maybe I should date Caleb and let the tongues wag. If you don't think anyone would suspect the truth about Caleb and Danny, maybe I've been overly concerned about nothing.''

"Even if the truth coming out about Danny's true paternity isn't an issue, are you so eager to get your heart broken again that you'd actually have an affair with Caleb?''

"I think Caleb is only interested in me because I made it perfectly clear that I wouldn't sleep with him. I must be the first woman who's ever said no, so he considers me a challenge. Maybe if I date him and—"

"You're going to sleep with him to discourage him? My heavens, Sheila, what are you thinking?"

"I'm thinking that maybe I should call and ask him out. Maybe I should throw caution to the wind and—"

The telephone on Sheila's desk rang. Both women gasped.

Sheila lifted the receiver. "Hanley's Garage and Tow Truck Service."

"Hi, Sheila."

Her stomach filled with butterflies at the sound of Caleb's voice. "Hello."

"How are you?" he asked.

"Fine. You?"

"I'm in need of a date for next Saturday night," he said. "It seems the town's throwing this big party at the country club in my honor. I thought maybe you'd like to go with me."

"I—I—" Quit stuttering, you idiot! she admonished herself. Here's your chance to catch the brass ring. "Yes."

"Yes?"

"Yes, I'd very much like to be your date for next Saturday night."

"Great. I'll pick you up around seven." He paused for a moment, then said, "What's your favorite flower?"

"My favorite—? White daisies."

"White daisies, huh? Yeah, they suit you."

"Danny said that you've stopped by and watched the Bulldogs practice nearly every day," Sheila said. "He was disappointed you didn't make it to the last couple of games."

"I thought it best to put a little space between Danny and me. That's what you wanted, isn't it?"

What she wanted? To put space between Danny and Caleb. Yes, that *was* what she wanted, wasn't it?

"You understand why I was afraid Danny might become too attached to you, don't you?" She glanced over the desk at Susan, who nibbled on her fries and tried to pretend she wasn't listening to every word of the private conversation.

"Yeah, I understand."

"Will I…will we see you before Saturday night?"

"Probably not," he said. "I'm going to spend a couple of days over in Marshallton with Spence Rand. We're going to do some fishing. But I'll be back in time to clean up real good for the country club. See you then, honey."

"Yes, see you then." Sheila hung up the receiver.

"He wants you to be his date for the big country club celebration, doesn't he?" Susan dropped the half-full bag of fries on the table. "If you ask me, you're begging for trouble by encouraging him."

"I didn't ask you, did I!"

"Gosh, Sheila, don't jump down my throat. I just can't bear to see you get hurt again. Remember, I was around the first time and I know what you went through when you found out you were pregnant with Danny."

"I'm not that foolish, scared young girl anymore," Sheila said. "Maybe Caleb isn't that same selfish, cocky young boy, either."

"I think I have on too much makeup." Sheila peered into the mirror over the dresser in her bedroom. "Y'all have got me looking like a painted doll!" She pulled a tissue from the decorative box on the oak dresser.

"Don't you dare!" Donna Fields warned. "I spent twenty minutes getting your makeup just right."

"You look perfect," Susan Redman assured her. "As a matter of fact, I've never seen you look better."

"Yeah, I know," Sheila told her friends. "That's the problem. I don't look like myself. Caleb will laugh himself silly when he sees me."

"When Caleb sees you, he'll drool all over himself," Donna said. "You are absolutely stunning in that dress. It was made for your long, well-proportioned body."

Sheila tugged on the just-above-the-knee hemline of her little black dress—a dress with a designer label that Donna had borrowed from a wealthy friend. The silk material clung perfectly to Sheila's statuesque frame, accenting her small waist. The neckline was quite modest, revealing nothing but her long, slender neck, whereas the back of the bodice plunged dramatically to her waist, exposing a wide expanse of skin.

"I feel naked in this thing." Sheila glanced over her shoulder into the mirror at the reflection of her bare back.

"You're chic," Susan said.

"You need one more thing to pull this look together." Donna rummaged in her purse, pulled out a satin box and flipped the lid.

"Wow!" Sheila and Susan said simultaneously when they saw the diamond and ruby earrings.

"Here, put these on." Donna lifted the dime-size earrings from their case and handed them to Sheila.

"Are they real?" Susan asked.

"Yes, they're real," Donna said.

"Whose are they?" Sheila gazed down at the shimmery circles in her hand. The most expensive piece of jewelry she'd ever owned was the hundred dollar wedding band Daniel had put on her finger the day they married.

"They're mine." Donna walked up behind Sheila, lifted her wavy chin-length hair behind her ears, then turned her to face the mirror again. "They're the perfect finishing touch. Now, go ahead and put them on. Susan and I have to get out of here before Caleb shows up."

With trembling fingers, Sheila removed the tiny gold

studs from her ears and replaced them with the borrowed jewels. "Is that really me?" she asked as she gazed into the mirror. "I feel like such a fraud."

"Stop putting yourself down," Donna said. "You're a lovely woman who never does anything with herself. It's past time you started making the most of what you've got. And believe me, Ms. Vance, you've got plenty."

"But do I have enough for someone like Caleb Bishop?"

"More than enough," Susan said, hugging her. "If the man has sense enough to realize it."

Caleb had practically dropped the bouquet of daisies when Sheila opened the door and invited him into her home. He wasn't sure what he'd been expecting, but it hadn't been the breathtakingly elegant woman whose loveliness had left him momentarily speechless. What had happened to the woman in overalls and no makeup? he'd wondered. For a split second he'd thought the stunning lady was another woman.

Boy, oh, boy, was Crooked Oak in for a surprise tonight. He'd known the busybodies would have gossip material for a week after he arrived at the country club with Sheila, but now they'd have a heyday discussing the widow's transformation from plain Jane to beauty queen.

He didn't know when he had looked forward to anything so much as he did escorting Sheila this evening or when he'd been so thoroughly fascinated by the prospect of seducing a woman. And he had every intention of, later tonight, using all his charm to entice Sheila into his bed.

"Ready?" Caleb asked Sheila when they entered the country club.

"As ready as I'll ever be," she said.

He slipped his arm around her waist and guided her into the fray. Every head turned. Soft whispers rose to loud murmurs. Half a dozen men, including the mayor, scurried toward them. And all the females in the room craned their necks to get a better view of the couple.

"Who's that with him?" one elderly matron inquired of her daughter.

"Good Lord, Mama, that's Sheila Vance."

"Can't be."

"It is Sheila Vance," another lady at their table said.

"Who'd ever have thought she was hiding a body like that under those overalls she wears," a man said, apologizing for his comment after his wife poked him in the ribs.

Sheila was unaccustomed to being the focus of so much attention. And even though she realized that Caleb was the man of the hour, she couldn't help but notice the way the men gathered around him kept glancing appreciatively in her direction. Did she really look that good? Had Susan and Donna been right? Was she truly lovely tonight?

"Sheila, my dear girl." Mayor Frost clasped her hand. "You look downright gorgeous."

Blushing profusely, she smiled shyly. "Thank you."

"Come along, Caleb. We have a table reserved up front for you and your date." Councilman Witten nodded toward the raised dais that had been set up, where the guest of honor would be put on display.

Knowing every eye in the house was focused on Caleb and her, Sheila was more nervous than she'd ever been in her entire life. Caleb might be accustomed to being the center of attention, but she wasn't. Most of her life she'd been a nonentity, a wallflower, a quiet, *sweet* girl no one gave a second glance.

The meal might have been delicious. She had no way of knowing. With her nerves tied in knots and a queasy feeling attacking her stomach, what little food she consumed tasted a great deal like cardboard. Grateful when the waiter carried away her untouched dessert, Sheila turned her attention to Mayor Frost as he gave Caleb a glowing introduction fit for a head of state.

With that familiar cocky smile in place, Caleb rose to the podium. He was, without a doubt, the most gorgeous hunk on God's green earth. The tuxedo he wore fit his body to perfection, accentuating the breadth of his wide shoulders and the slimness of his hips. Before he even opened his mouth to speak, his presence alone mesmerized the crowd.

Sheila noticed the way he kept his right arm down by his side and used his left hand while he spoke. Knowing that the partial paralysis in his pitching arm and hand was irreversible had to torment him on a daily basis. He had gone from the highest paid, most famous baseball player in the world to a has-been. Few men could endure such a loss without becoming angry and bitter. Tallie had told her about the horrible days and nights after the accident, when she had sat by her brother's bedside, not knowing whether he would live or die. And when he had regained consciousness and learned about his disability, he'd told his sister that he wished he had died.

"Folks, what can I say?" Caleb's gaze moved across the jam-packed room. "It's good to be home."

The deafening applause rocked the country club. One by one the attendees rose from their seats to pay tribute to Crooked Oak's hometown hero—one of their own who had skyrocketed to superstardom in the athletic world.

Sheila saw the muscle in Caleb's jaw tighten and watched as he took a deep breath. A fine sheen of moisture coated his eyes. She wanted to jump up and put her arms around him, to tell him it was all right, that if he needed to cry, to just go ahead and cry. Instead, she sat there as he struggled to control his emotions, knowing that he wouldn't succumb to the feelings rioting inside him. Big, tough, macho man. No tears for him. No show of weakness in front of his adoring fans.

Caleb lifted his arm and motioned for the audience to

PLAY
"PINBALL WIZ"
10
5
15
Scratch the silver circles and claim
2 FREE BOOKS
AND A FREE GIFT!
See inside

No risk, no obligation to buy...now or ever!

HOW TO PLAY

"PINBALL WIZ"

and be eligible to receive

THREE FREE GIFTS!

1. With a coin, carefully scratch the silver circles on the opposite page. Then, including the numbers on the front of this card, count up your total pinball score and check the claim chart to see what we have for you. **2 FREE** books and a **FREE** gift!

2. Send back this card and you'll receive brand-new Silhouette Desire® novels. These books have a cover price of $3.75 each in the U.S. and $4.25 each in Canada, but they are yours to keep absolutely **FREE**!

3. There's no catch. You're under no obligation to buy anything. We charge you nothing for your first shipment. And you don't have to make a minimum number of purchases — not even one!

4. The fact is, thousands of readers enjoy receiving books by mail from the Silhouette Reader Service®. They like the convenience of home delivery and they like getting the best new novels before they're available in stores...and they love our discount prices!

5. We hope that after receiving your free books you'll want to remain a subscriber. But the choice is yours -— to continue or cancel, anytime at all! So why not take us up on our invitation, with no risk of any kind.
You'll be glad you did!

FREE
MYSTERY GIFT!

We can't tell you what it is...but we're sure you'll like it! A free gift just for accepting our **NO-RISK** offer!

take their seats. "I never realized when I left Crooked Oak, how far my love for baseball would take me."

"It took you all the way to the top," a male voice called from the back of the room. "You're a real legend, Caleb Bishop, and this whole town is proud of you."

Caleb smiled, amazing Sheila once again with his knack for charming a crowd. As he spoke about his career, he had the townsfolk on the edge of their seats. And when he briefly mentioned the accident that had ended his brilliant career, he brought a tear to every eye—except his own.

The mayor awarded Caleb a key to the city and a huge plaque honoring his accomplishments. After the audience gave another round of thundering applause for the guest of honor, the band struck up a soothing melody and several couples filtered out onto the dance floor.

Pumping Caleb's hand, Mayor Frost patted him on the back. "We're so proud to have you home in Crooked Oak, son."

After thanking each and every citizen who surrounded him for a personal congratulatory handshake, Caleb turned to Sheila and held out his hand.

"Care to dance, lovely lady?"

Smiling, her heart filled with love, Sheila rose from her chair and accepted his hand. He led her out onto the dance floor and brought her into his embrace. He danced with the same eloquence with which he spoke. Confident and practiced. At first, she felt awkward, but within minutes she lost herself in the moment, in the sheer joy of being in Caleb's arms.

"You're the most beautiful woman here tonight," he whispered in her ear.

Her heart soared, even though her mind warned her not to believe his compliment. What would it hurt, she asked herself, if just for tonight she believed him? If just for tonight she could pretend to be beautiful and desirable and the only woman in the world Caleb wanted?

He'll break your heart again, an inner voice cautioned. *He'll take all that you offer him, give you hope where there is none and then he'll leave you. A woman like you could never hold a man like Caleb Bishop.*

She ached for him, in that age-old hungry way a woman's body longs to be filled, to be taken and ravished, to be claimed by the one man destined to be her mate. No other man had ever made her feel the way Caleb did. He and he alone could fulfill her most basic needs.

During the dances he shared with other women that night, she was kept busy by a continual flow of eager partners. Men who'd never given her the time of day before, laughed and flirted with her. Did she look that good? Or were they all lining up for a dance with Caleb Bishop's date?

By the time the evening drew to a close, Caleb made his way back to her and pulled her into his arms for the last dance. This evening had been a dream come true for her. Twelve years ago she had attended her senior prom with Elbert Platt, the biggest nerd in school, and had watched Caleb dance with a succession of pretty girls. Although he'd spoken to her and bestowed his beautiful smile on her, he hadn't asked her to dance. Not once. But tonight, she was the belle of the ball. Tonight she was Caleb's date.

Later, after farewells to his hometown fans, Caleb drove Sheila out of Crooked Oak and onto the road that led to her home and, farther out, his family farm.

"Are you sure you don't mind if we ride with the top down?" he asked.

"Why should I mind? It's a warm, glorious spring night." She leaned her head back against the plush leather seat.

"Most women wouldn't want the wind to mess up their hair." He glanced over at Sheila and once again marveled at how truly lovely she was. In reality, the makeup and clothes and the slightly different hairstyle hadn't changed the woman, they had simply enhanced a good body and fine bone structure.

"I'm not most women," she said.

"I've finally realized that."

They drove in silence, the warm night breeze ruffling their hair and caressing their skin. Caleb slowed the Porsche as he neared the exit to Sheila's house.

"Since Danny's spending the night with Tanner Finch, there's no reason for you to go home now, is there?" *Take this slow and easy,* he warned himself. *Don't rush her. Don't push her.* "We could drive over to Marshallton to one of the clubs."

"I'm not much of a party girl," she told him. "But if that's what you'd really like to do, then—"

"What I'd really like to do is take you home with me." He stopped the car in front of her house, but didn't kill the motor.

"Are you trying to ask me to spend the night with you?"

"Yeah, I guess I am."

"Then ask me."

As he turned to her, he laid his arm across the back of her seat and leaned over so that they were face-to-face. "I'd like to take you home with me and spend the night making love to you."

"All right."

"All right?" He stared at her in disbelief. Had he heard her correctly or had he imagined her reply?

"Are you saying that you'll—"

She covered his lips with her index finger, silencing him immediately. "I'm saying that I want you to make love to me all night long."

"What changed your mind?" He nibbled on the tip of her finger.

My need to be with the only man I've ever loved. "I decided it might be worth the risk." And as he gazed deeply into her eyes, she realized something else. That she was willing to take the chance that this time, they could give each other what they both needed. That this time Caleb would want to stay with her. With her and their son.

He lowered his head and kissed her. Soft, sweet and tender beyond belief, as if he were handling a fragile object that could be broken easily. She sighed as tingling awareness spread from her core throughout her entire body.

Caleb lifted his head quickly, took a deep breath and grinned. "No more of that or we'll be making out in the car."

"Like we did twelve years ago," she said.

"This isn't going to be like it was twelve years ago," he promised. "This time we're going to be in my bed and I'm going to love you like you've never been loved. And when morning comes, we're not going to regret one moment we shared."

Her breath caught in her throat. He revved the motor and sped the Porsche down the road toward the Bishop farm. Within five minutes, he parked the car in the driveway, got out, rounded the hood and jerked open the passenger door. After shoving the keys into his pants' pocket, he reached for her. Hurriedly, he pulled her from the car and into his arms. She went willingly, happily, delirious with the prospect of what lay ahead for them.

Together they raced up to the porch. Caleb shoved her against the front door and kissed her until she couldn't breathe. With unsteady fingers, she removed his bow tie and undid the tiny buttons on his pleated shirt. He cupped her hip and lifted her up against his arousal.

Their tongues participated in a primeval foreplay dance that excited both his senses and hers. He reached into his pocket, pulled out his key chain, inserted the house key into the lock and opened the door. Kissing, clinging, ripping off each other's clothes, they made their way inside. Caleb kicked the front door closed.

They made a trail, consisting of a tuxedo jacket, a white shirt, a pair of high heels and a black silk dress, from the living room to Caleb's bedroom. Now there was no turning back from their appointment with destiny.

Seven

Caleb fumbled with the catch on her bra. "Damn! I can't seem to maneuver this with my left hand, honey." He nipped her neck playfully.

With no doubts or fears, Sheila unhooked the catch of her strapless long-line bra, then allowed Caleb to remove the garment. After dropping the bra to the floor, he held Sheila by one arm, stepped back and surveyed her naked breasts. Aroused and pleased by the sight of her, he sucked in his breath.

She had such lovely breasts. Round and full. Lush without being large. Pink diamond peaks that beckoned his mouth.

His sex hardened. His heart raced. "I want to see all of you," he said. "Every beautiful inch."

She nodded, knowing what he wanted her to do, all the while praying he would not find her thirty-year-old body lacking. She didn't possess the firm body of an eighteen-year-old any longer and her stomach bore the faint scars of pregnancy.

Calling upon all her courage and driven by her desire for this man, she moved away from him and began a slow, uncertain striptease. First, she eased the black pantyhose down her legs, then sat on the edge of the bed and slid them over her feet. Her hands shook when she reached for the lace waistband of her black panties.

Caleb watched her every move, waiting eagerly for the unveiling.

Sheila stood by the bed, and inch by slow, torturous inch, slipped the panties down her hips and legs. When they dropped to her ankles, she kicked them aside. Then she lifted her head and looked directly at him. He smiled, wickedly, sensually, and moved toward her. She trembled from head to toe when he reached out and touched her throat with his fingertips.

"That first time, in the car twelve years ago, I didn't really look at you," he said.

She swallowed hard. "I—I know. It was dark in your car."

"Lady, you've got the greatest pair of legs I've ever seen. Damn, they're a mile long." He ran his fingertip downward, between her breasts, across her belly and into her navel.

She took in a deep breath. "You like—"

"Everything I see," he assured her as he opened his palm and smoothed it down and over her mound. "Now I want to touch and taste what I'm looking at right now." He slid his hand between her legs, urged her thighs apart and massaged her intimately.

Her knees weakened and she suddenly felt very lightheaded. As he continued the assault on her sensitive kernel, her femininity clenched and unclenched, tightening and loosening in preparation. Desire spiraled through her, creating a ravenous longing inside her. When he inserted a couple of his fingers up into the moist depths of her body, she flung back her head and moaned.

"You're so hot and wet." He growled the words as he lowered his mouth to her breast.

"Caleb!" His name came out on a gasping cry.

She swayed on her feet. He gave her a gentle nudge and she fell backward onto the bed. He came down on top of her, straddling her hips. When he kissed her, she responded by opening her mouth to the invasion of his tongue. The moment he took possession of her mouth, she bucked her hips off the bed, pressing her mound against his throbbing arousal.

As she squirmed beneath him, he petted the soft curls at the apex of her thighs and urged her to part her legs once more. He began anew the seduction of her senses, stroking, probing, rubbing, slipping in and out, while his mouth moved from one begging nipple to the other. He lavished attention on each jutted point, laving, sucking, nibbling.

The heat built inside her to the boiling point, threatening to explode at any moment. He encouraged her to achieve fulfillment, with every caress of his fingers, each lick of his tongue. She had never known anything so unbearably intense, so incredibly wild, so completely uncontrollable. She was lost in a world of sensation, consumed by Caleb's masterful touch. With one final flick of his tongue across her breast, one last perfect pressure to her core, Caleb released the pleasure inside her. She cried out, stunned by the power of her climax.

Leaving her briefly, Caleb divested himself of his tuxedo pants and black briefs. With a quick, hard thrust he entered her and for one brief instant he thought he would die from the pleasure. Nothing had ever been this good. This right.

Sheila wrapped her long legs around him and urged him to take his own pleasure. He rode her hard, like a madman, crazed by passion. She clung to his shoulders as the bed shook from the force of his lunges. With each repeated attack, her body tightened more and more, trying to hold on to the bucking bronc, seeking once again the ultimate sensation.

He mumbled rough, crude words in her ear. And when he hammered into her, she shivered as she unraveled with her second release. Caleb convulsed with the throes of completion, his big body shaking as he uttered a long, low, animalistic groan.

Dropping to her side on the bed, he threw his arm across her belly. She laid her hand over his. As his chest rose and fell with the rapid beat of his heart, he sighed contentedly. Sheila cuddled her head against his shoulder.

He kissed her damp forehead. "That was incredible," he said. "You were incredible. And you loved it, didn't you, honey?"

"Yes." She hid her face against his shoulder.

"I don't know how much experience you've had," he said, "but I guess you know that it isn't always like that. Not always that powerful."

"It's been a long time for me," she told him. "I suppose I was long overdue."

"Yeah, it's been a while for me, too. But something tells me that when we do it again, it'll be just as good. Maybe better."

"Do it again?" She lifted her head and gazed into his twinkling black eyes.

He speared his fingers through the dusty blond curls covering her mound. "I want you to stay all night, remember? I don't think either one of us has appeased our appetite yet, do you? I figure we'll both be hungry again before morning."

He eased his arm under her, clasping her shoulder. She snuggled against him and closed her eyes. She'd never known anything so absolutely perfect as the feel of his body next to hers.

* * *

Caleb woke slowly, languidly, and found a woman in his bed. But not just any woman, he thought. Sheila. He smiled when he recalled how Sheila had given herself to him with wild abandon, holding back nothing, reveling in the pure, honest emotions he had evoked from her. She didn't possess the smooth, practiced wiles of the more experienced women he'd bedded, and that pleased him. There had been nothing lacking in the experience they'd shared. Raw, primitive and fully satisfying, their lovemaking had been the sweetest thing he'd ever known.

The light they'd left on in the living room spread down the hallway and shed a pale, hazy glow over the bedroom. He glanced at the bedside clock. Four-fifteen. It would be daybreak soon and the night would end. And Sheila would leave him.

He eased the sheet from her body, exposing her breasts. He wondered if she had breast-fed Danny, and an unexpected tinge of jealousy jolted him at the thought that it had been Daniel Vance who had been Sheila's husband for seven years. That he had been the man to whom she had given her body and her heart—the man who had fathered her child. Caleb knew he had no right to envy a dead man and yet on some primordial level, he did. He felt that Sheila was his now and he wanted to claim her completely, and along with her, her son. He had assured her that he wouldn't allow Danny to become overly attached to him, but how the hell was he going to pursue a relationship with the mother without including the child?

He'd never had an ongoing relationship with a woman who had a kid, so this was a first for him. When he put his life back together and knew what he was going to do for the next twenty or thirty years, he'd leave Crooked Oak behind, the way he had twelve years ago. And the one thing he didn't want, the one thing he had to prevent, was hurting Sheila and Danny when he left. He would continue being honest with both of them. He wanted to be Sheila's lover and Danny's friend, but he couldn't make a commitment to them, nothing beyond the present.

Apparently Sheila had changed her mind and was willing to accept a short-term affair; otherwise, she wouldn't be here with him right now.

Caleb pulled the sheet away from her body, revealing her broad hips and long legs...and the soft, thick triangle of curls. His sex hardened and longing raced through his bloodstream. She possessed a woman's body, natural in every aspect. Imperfect and yet beautiful.

More than anything in the world, he wanted to make love to her again, to ease the ache of desire building steadily inside him.

He kissed her shoulder. She didn't stir. He licked the same spot. She stirred slightly. He gently nipped her skin. She moaned.

Caleb slipped his hand between her thighs as he leaned over and drew one soft nipple into his mouth.

Sheila's eyelids fluttered. "Caleb?"

He suckled her breast and massaged her core. Taking in a deep, startled breath, she opened her eyes.

"Caleb, what—"

He lifted his head from her breast, brought his lips to hers and took her mouth with searing intensity. Her sex dampened and throbbed as he ravaged her mouth and continued the delicate probe of her body. Her breasts swelled as heat spread through her veins.

Sheila opened her mouth, inviting him into the warmth. He accepted the invitation, plunging his tongue inside and drinking the sweetness. When she tried to pull him to her, urging him to mount her, he refused her nonverbal request. Instead he deepened the kiss and increased the speed of his plundering fingers.

She realized that he intended to pleasure her before taking her, so she gave herself over to him, accepting his command. He sucked at her lips, nibbling and tasting, while his talented fingers caressed with ever-growing urgency. The tension within her coiled tighter and tighter, taking her deeper and deeper into the darkness. Caleb licked a line from her mouth to her chest, slowly, patiently, as if he had all the time in the world. When his tongue touched her pebble-hard nipple, she cried out from the pleasurable pain and plunged to the very depths of sensation. Then the spring of pleasure inside her snapped and uncoiled, bringing her upward. Higher and higher. She writhed and moaned and completely fell apart.

While ripples of completion echoed through her body, Caleb lifted her up and over him. With her legs straddling him, she took the dominant position. Gazing down at him through passion-filled eyes, Sheila visually devoured him. Bronze skin taut over hard muscles, black curling chest hair and dark rosy-brown nipples. She felt his thick, heavy arousal pulsing beneath her.

She wanted him inside her, filling her, stretching her, giving her even more pleasure. Maneuvering her hand between her thighs, she reached out and circled his stiff sex. He moaned when she touched him. She guided him into her and took him completely, straining to bury him deeply. He grabbed her hips and bucked upward, impaling her.

She cried out, tossed back her head and clutched his shoulders. As he began a steady rhythmic undulation, he caressed her buttocks, then grasped them and taught her the rhythm. She leaned into him, offering him her breasts. Lifting his head, he washed first one and then the other begging nipple, leaving both tight and damp. She changed the pace, taking complete control and setting the tone for their lovemaking. He acquiesced to her wishes, quickly adapting to the slow, pounding massage that led them closer and closer to the edge.

As the sensual dance progressed, she quickened the pace to a brutal frenzy. Release hit her hard, rocking her body with its force. She cried and moaned and twisted, draining every ounce of fulfillment from her body. Caleb tumbled her over onto her back and hammered into her repeatedly, then clenched his teeth tightly, groaning, shivering, crying out, as he jetted into her.

Holding her close, he covered her face with kisses. "Ah, Sheila, Sheila."

Morning sunshine flooded the room through the eastern windows. Sheila found herself alone in the bed. She lifted her head from the pillow and glanced at the clock. Eight-thirty. She never slept this late, not even on the weekends.

Before she had a chance to call out his name, Caleb, wearing nothing but his black briefs, came through the door, a tray in his hands and a warm smile on his face.

"It's a great day," he said. "Sunny and bright. Not a cloud in the sky." He brought the tray over to the bed and set it in Sheila's lap, then dropped down beside her and kissed her soundly on the lips.

When he stared at her naked breasts, she tugged on the sheet, bringing it up to cover her. "What's this?"

"This—" he nodded to the tray "—is breakfast. Coffee and toast. That's about the extent of my culinary abilities."

Sheila lifted one of the cups, took a sip and smiled. "Not bad."

He leaned over and kissed her shoulder. "Can you stay all day?"

"All day?"

"We haven't even begun to explore all the possibilities, all the variations, all the—"

She placed her index finger across his lips. "I'm tempted. Really, I am. But Danny will be expecting me to meet him at church. I told Teresa Finch that I'd take Tanner and Danny to a movie this afternoon, after I treat them to lunch at Pete's."

"So, you're going to throw me over in favor of two younger guys, huh?" Caleb nuzzled her neck.

"You could come along," she said. "Pete's has a great Sunday buffet and—"

"Do you think it's a good idea for me to do the *family* thing with you and Danny?" Caleb lifted the other cup off the tray. Holding it with both hands, he sipped the hot, strong coffee. Eyeing her over the rim of the cup, he waited for her response.

Sheila reached for a piece of toast. "I know that lunch and a movie with two eleven-year-old boys is hardly your idea of an exciting Sunday afternoon, but I thought you might actually enjoy being with us."

He set the cup down on the tray, clasped Sheila's chin in his hand and tilted her head up. "Look at me, honey," he began, "other than spending the day right here in bed with you, I can't think of anything I'd rather do than have lunch at Pete's and take the boys to a movie over in Marshallton. It's just that I didn't want you worrying about Danny and me getting really tight."

"Maybe I was wrong about that," she said. *I'm hoping and praying I was wrong. I want to believe that you're not the same selfish boy you once were, that you're a mature man with the ability to give as well as take.*

"I'd like to be a part of yours and Danny's lives," Caleb said. "I don't want last night to be another one-night stand for us."

"Neither do I," she said, moving her chin out of his grasp and casting her gaze downward.

"I won't make any promises that I can't keep," he told her. "But I don't won't to lose what we've found. We're good together, Sheila. I mean, really good." He caressed her cheek. "And I don't mean just in bed, although that's fantastic. I mean, we like each other. We enjoy each other's company. I haven't had all of that with other women."

Leaning her head against his cheek, she captured his hand between them and pressed her lips against his knuckles. "I'll try not to ask for too much too soon, but I have to admit that I want more than a brief affair."

She wondered if she should be so honest with him, if her frankness would scare him away. If only she could tell him that she loved him, had never stopped loving him. If only she could trust him to accept Danny and her into his life completely and commit himself to them. If she could trust him wholeheartedly, she could tell him that Danny was his son.

Caleb lifted the tray and placed it on the floor, then pulled the sheet away from her body and shoved her gently back into the bed. "Let's work on the brief affair first, honey, and then we'll see what happens."

"Caleb!" she protested, but not very vehemently. "I need to go home, take a bath and get ready for church."

"You've got plenty of time." He whipped off his briefs and tossed them to the floor.

"But it's already—"

He covered her body with his and took her mouth in a silencing kiss. She struggled against him momentarily, then her traitorous body took charge and she was lost. Without even the pretense of foreplay, he rammed into her and sighed gruffly as he embedded himself deeply.

Sheila responded passionately, afire with her own needs. Needs that had gone unfulfilled for far too many years.

While Caleb was in the shower, the telephone rang. Sheila, who had already bathed and put on the black dress she'd worn the night before, hesitated. If she answered, whoever was calling would know she was at Caleb's house early on a Sunday morning and would probably assume correctly that she'd spent the night. Deciding to allow the answering machine to respond, she picked up her heels and slipped into them.

"Caleb, if you're there, answer the phone," the male voice said. "I've got a proposition for you I think you're going to like. How would you like to live in Greenville, South Carolina? Give me a call ASAP, and I'll fill you in on the details.''

Sheila froze to the spot. How would Caleb like to live in Greenville, South Carolina? What was in Greenville? And who was the man making the proposition? Her heart sank. Surely Caleb wouldn't leave Crooked Oak so soon. He'd been here only a few weeks. Not long enough. Not nearly long enough.

Long enough for what? she asked herself. He's been here long enough for you to fall under his spell again, for you to give him your heart and your body and your very soul. Long enough for you to start hoping for the impossible again!

"Who was that on the phone?" Caleb asked as he emerged from the bathroom, a towel wrapped around his lean hips.

"I didn't answer," she said. "He left a message."

"What sort of message?"

Sheila hit the button on the answering machine. "Hear for yourself."

Caleb instantly recognized Dale Harris's baritone drawl. His agent for most of his career, Dale had stood by Caleb after the accident and proved himself a real friend.

The minute Dale mentioned Greenville, Caleb suspected what the proposition was. One of the Braves's minor league teams was home-based in Greenville and there were rumors that A. J. Macias, the team's coach, was thinking about retiring.

"That's my agent, Dale Harris," Caleb told her. "Would you mind if I give him a quick call before I drive you home?"

"I can walk home. It isn't that far."

"Absolutely not. I'm driving you home to change and then we're going to church together and—"

"Make your phone call, first," she said. "You might have to change your plans after you talk to your agent."

"Nothing's going to change my plans for today." He crossed the room hurriedly, grabbed her arm and pulled her up against his chest. "Nothing takes priority over my spending time with you today." He kissed her nose. "Have you got that?"

She nodded shyly, bowing her head as feelings of doubt churned in her stomach and uncertainties crept into her mind. She wanted to believe that today was the beginning of a whole new life for her, for Caleb and for Danny. But now her fears cautioned her that she'd been overly optimistic to think she had a future with Caleb.

With his hand around her waist, Caleb pulled her along as he walked across the room, sat on the bed and picked up the telephone. He hauled her onto his lap, lifted her arm and draped it around his neck. "Stay put, honey. This won't take long."

She sat there stiffly, her heart racing, her nerves screaming, as Caleb dialed a number he obviously had memorized. When a male voice answered the call, she leaned her head against Caleb's and waited quietly for him to speak.

"What's this about a proposition I'm going to like?" Caleb asked.

Sheila heard Dale Harris's voice on the other end of the line. "It's definite. A.J. is going to retire in two years and he's told the owners that he'd like to turn the team over to you. They want to talk to you about it, feel you out to see if you're interested. I told them we'd let them know something tomorrow."

"Two years is a long time to wait for a job," Caleb said. "I'll go out of my mind with nothing to do until A.J. retires."

"Hey, I as good as told them that and…" Dale paused for effect. "They suggested you might want to work alongside A.J. as an assistant coach for the next couple of years."

"That's a possibility that interests me, but not nearly as much as the head coaching position." Caleb nuzzled Sheila's neck. She kissed his temple. "How about I drive over to Atlanta tomorrow and we ask them to put us an offer on the table?"

"I knew you'd say that," Dale replied. "So I've set up a tentative meeting for two tomorrow afternoon. And A.J.'s expecting you to meet the guys on the Greenville Braves and see how y'all connect."

"Can't say I hoped I'd be coaching by the time I was thirty." Caleb chuckled, the sound mixed with regret and resignation. "I'd thought it was something I'd be doing when I was well over forty. But at least a coaching job would keep me in the game."

"Why don't you drive on over today and spend the night with Shelby and me?" Dale suggested.

"Can't." Caleb squeezed Sheila's hip. "I've got more important things to do today. See you tomorrow."

As soon as Caleb hung up the receiver, Sheila slid off his lap and stood by the bed. "I'd understand if you want to drive to Atlanta today."

He reached out, took her hands in his and lifted them to his lips. Kissing her hands repeatedly, he made an effort to reassure her. "I want to spend the day with you."

She forced a smile, all the while her heart warned her to beware. "I couldn't help but overhear everything. About the coaching position with the minor league team."

"Yeah, it's great, isn't it, honey? I'm not sure it's what I want to do, but at least it gives me an option that would enable me to stay connected to the game."

"If you decide to take the position as an assistant coach, when would you begin work?"

"I don't know." He stood and put his arm around her shoulders. "Probably right away. Spring training has already started."

"If you take the job, then you'd be moving right away, wouldn't you?"

"Yeah, I'd have to." Noticing the forlorn look on Sheila's face, he tickled her chin, then lifted it, urging her to look directly at him. "Nothing's settled. We haven't even discussed terms, yet. I might not want the assistant's job. I could find something else to occupy my time until A.J. retires and his position is available."

She wanted to scream, *But what about us?* and then realized that there was no *us*. An affair, no matter what the duration, was not a commitment. It wasn't an offer of marriage, and only marriage would ever tie Caleb to her permanently. Whether he left Crooked Oak now or in two weeks or two years, the results would more than likely be the same. When it came time for him to move on, Caleb would leave her and Danny behind and she'd be left to pick up the pieces of her shattered life.

Their idyllic Sunday ended far too soon and Monday morning rolled over her like a steam engine, full speed ahead. After church, they'd eaten at Pete's Café and driven over to Marshallton to the movies. Then Caleb had played catch with Danny and Tanner until dusk and the Finches and Susan and Lowell had stopped by to join them for homemade ice cream.

And after they'd put Danny to bed, she and Caleb had sneaked off outside and made love in a wooded grove behind the house. He had left her, reluctantly, at midnight, but she hadn't slept until nearly dawn.

She stood on the back porch, watching the rain come down in a slow, steady springtime shower. Was Caleb up and getting ready to leave for Atlanta? Or had he left already? Would he think of her while he was gone? Would their relationship affect any of the decisions he made about his future?

The dampness blew onto the porch, a fine mist caressing

her face and bare arms. She shivered as the cool moisture touched her.

The telephone rang. She gasped, startled by the unexpected sound. She raced into the kitchen, lifted the receiver from the wall and held her breath.

"Hello?"

"Good morning, sunshine," Caleb said.

"Good morning, yourself." Her heart beat against her chest like a trapped bird.

"I'm fixing to head out, but I wanted to hear your voice one more time."

"I'm so glad you called," she told him. "Please, drive carefully. The roads will be slick and dangerous because of the rain."

"Don't worry about me. I'll be fine. I'll miss you while I'm gone."

"I'll miss you, too."

"I shouldn't be gone long. Three or four days at most. And when I come back, we might have something to celebrate."

She wanted to beg him to come back to her and never leave her, ever again. But she could hardly do that. Despite what they'd shared, she had no claim on Caleb. She never had and probably never would. She needed to start the process now, while she still could. She had to let Caleb go— in her mind and in her heart. He might come back to Crooked Oak. He might return to her temporarily. But in the end, he would go away and leave her again.

End it now! End it now! her mind shouted. *Do it before it's too late and you ruin your life and Danny's by trying to hold on to something that never belonged to you in the first place.*

"Caleb, I—" She couldn't! Heaven help her, she couldn't. Not if there was one chance in a million. "Come home soon."

"As soon as I can, honey. Believe me, as soon as I can."

Eight

Caleb gave the Realtor a check and the two shook hands. For the first time in years, he knew, for sure and certain, that he was doing the right thing. The coaching job in Greenville would be his in two years, if he still wanted it, and he figured that by then he'd know for sure which would be the best route for him to take. As much as he loved baseball, he really didn't see himself playing assistant coach for twenty-four months, waiting around until A.J. retired. No, what he needed was enough time and space to adjust to his new status as a former athletic superstar. The best place for him was right here in Crooked Oak, where he would always be a hero to the locals.

He had to admit to himself that he wasn't sure how much of a part Sheila Vance played in his decision not to move to Greenville right now. All he knew was that the idea of not seeing Sheila on a regular basis didn't appeal to him in the least. In the two weeks he'd been away, she'd been on his mind day and night. And so had Danny. There was just something about Sheila and her son. Something special.

Was that what he really needed, what he truly wanted— a ready-made family? He'd been tempted to take the job in Greenville simply to escape his possessive feelings about Sheila and Danny. Never in a million years had he ever thought he'd be tempted to settle down in his old hometown with a widow and her child. Hell, he wasn't the settling-down type, wasn't the marrying kind. And he knew Sheila would expect nothing less than forever after. Was he willing to make that kind of a commitment?

He wasn't sure about anything, least of all his feelings about a future with Sheila. But by renting this downtown building and opening a baseball-card shop to fill the endless hours each day, he figured he could take all the time he needed to find out what he really wanted.

Caleb had made the decision yesterday when he'd stayed overnight with Dale and Shelby in Atlanta. And he'd called the Realtor first thing this morning. A certain sense of relief filled him now that he'd made some decisions about the next year. He was going to stay in Crooked Oak, open a baseball-card shop, fiddle around with restoring a few old cars and maybe even do a little farming. He wouldn't mind raising a few head of beef cattle and growing enough grain to feed them.

And he was going to court the Widow Vance. Caleb grinned. Hell, he was going to have a full-blown affair with the woman. He wanted her in his bed every night. Just the thought of the last time they'd made love gave him a rock-solid hard-on.

But he realized he'd probably have to mend a few fences with Sheila. He had kept in touch with her the first week he'd been out of town, but then, when he'd realized just how much the woman meant to him, he'd panicked and pulled back, hoping his feelings for her would change. He hadn't talked to her in a week and she was sure to be upset with him. He had to find a way to make her understand.

He wasn't used to caring so much about another person, to truly needing one specific woman in his life on a daily basis.

Caleb pocketed the keys to the building he'd just leased, exited the Realtor's office and slid behind the wheel of his Porsche. Should he go to the farm and settle in before he contacted Sheila, or should he go straight to the garage? If he called first, he gave her the opportunity to tell him she didn't want to see him. No, his best course of action was to go directly to her, face her wrath and then drag her out of the garage and straight to the nearest bed.

Sheila kicked the tire on the Honda, then winced when pain shot up her foot and leg. Damn! For the past week she'd been taking her frustration and anger out on any inanimate object available whenever thoughts of Caleb Bishop crossed her mind. That man! That inconsiderate, uncaring SOB! She should have known better. She wasn't some starry-eyed teenager any longer. Why hadn't she listened to her head instead of her heart? If she had, she wouldn't be hurting so much right now, and she wouldn't be so furious.

She hadn't heard a word from Caleb in a week. He had planned to be away only a few days. Those few days had turned into a week and then into two weeks. He probably wasn't ever coming back to Crooked Oak. And that was just fine and dandy with her. She didn't care if he never came back.

Liar! an inner voice mocked her. *You care. You care too damn much. You're dying inside and you know it. All your hopes and dreams have gone up in smoke. Caleb Bishop used you again. And left you, just as he did twelve years ago.*

Sheila slammed down the Honda's hood, dropped the wrench into her toolbox and pulled out a rag from the back pocket of her overalls. Tanya Tucker's gravelly voice belted out her latest country hit from the CD player at the back of the garage. Checking her watch, Sheila realized it was past lunchtime, nearly one. Her stomach growled.

She had a full afternoon ahead of her, with Mike gone for the rest of the day to accompany Christy to her doctor's appointment. Today the sonogram should reveal the sex of her brother's child, and he was beyond excited.

Wiping her hands on the orange rag, Sheila thought about her own pregnancy. She'd been eighteen, alone and scared. And Daniel Vance had been her rescuer, marrying her, loving her and giving her baby a father. What would she have done without him? No woman should go through a pregnancy alone, without her man at her side.

Caleb Bishop had missed out on one of life's most precious experiences.

Stop thinking about him! she admonished herself. Stop torturing yourself with what-ifs.

He's gone. Out of your life. And good riddance. He'd have been nothing but trouble for you and Danny.

Sheila washed up hurriedly, pulled her bologna sandwich and bag of chips out of the paper sack, poured herself a cup of hours-old coffee and propped her behind down on an uncluttered spot on her desk. While quickly devouring the sandwich and chips, she answered the phone twice. Once a wrong number. And once a customer checking on his car. Each time the phone rang, her heart jumped up in her throat. Stupid woman! she chided herself. Do you really think Caleb is going to call?

Just as she dumped the trash in the wastebasket, she heard a vehicle pull up outside the garage. Craning her neck to glance out the window, she saw Caleb's Porsche. Every muscle in her body froze.

What was he doing here? Had he come to say goodbye? Well, he needn't have bothered. She'd already said goodbye to him, already cut him out of her heart.

You're lying to yourself again, that little inner voice told her.

Oh, my gosh, she must look a fright. No makeup. Her

hair held off her face with a headband and her body encased in a pair of baggy overalls. She shouldn't care what he thought of her, but dammit, she did care.

She licked her lips. Caleb walked toward the front entrance. No time to even run a comb through her hair, she thought as he opened the office door. *Act nonchalant,* the voice advised. *As if you don't care that he's back in town, as if you aren't the least bit interested in anything he has to say.*

Caleb stepped over the threshold and hesitated.

"Hello, honey," he said in that deep, molasses-rich Southern baritone.

Despite her intentions to remain unaffected by his presence, she glared at him, a frown marring her features, "Hello, Caleb."

"Where's Mike? Looks like you're holding down the fort all by yourself today."

"Mike's with Christy. She's having a sonogram done today. They'll find out if the baby's a boy or girl."

"That's great." Caleb took a tentative step forward, then stopped abruptly when Sheila turned her back on him and headed out of the office and into the workstation. "I guess you're pretty busy, huh?"

"Very." *Go away, Caleb,* she wanted to scream. *Go away and leave me alone. I never want to see you again.*

"I know I should have called you this past week," he said as he followed her out into the garage. "But I wanted to wait until I'd made some definite decisions before I talked to you again."

"There's no reason for you to have called," she told him. "You didn't make me any promises. We don't have a commitment."

"You're angry, aren't you? I knew you would be. I'm sorry, honey. It's just that—"

Bracing her hands on her hips, she turned to face him, her eyes glimmering with rage. "Look, Caleb, just say what you have to say and then leave. Okay? You don't need to make any pretty speeches or try to soothe my feelings. You didn't bother with any of that nonsense twelve years ago and there's no reason for you to bother now."

"Do you want to sock me in the jaw? Would that make you feel better?" He turned his cheek and stuck out his chin.

"I don't want to hit you! I just want you to leave. Go away and don't ever bother me again."

Taking slow, steady steps in her direction, Caleb grinned, his smile curving the left side of his mouth. "I'm afraid I can't oblige you. I have no intention of going away. And I have plans to bother you a lot during the next year."

"What?" Had she heard him correctly? How could he bother her during the next year when he'd be hundreds of miles away in South Carolina?

"I honestly don't know what the future holds for you and me, but I'm going to stick around and find out." He neared her, only a couple of feet separating them.

"You—you're going to stick around? Here? In Crooked Oak?"

"Yep."

"But what about the coaching job in Greenville?"

Don't let your hopes soar. Don't start dreaming again.

"The job is mine in two years, if I still want it," Caleb said. "I decided against the assistant's job."

"You're going to stay in Crooked Oak for the next two years?"

Even if he stays, it doesn't mean he's staying because of you.

"For the next year, at least." He moved closer.

She backed away from him. "The next year?"

"Yeah, I just leased space downtown," he told her. "I'm going to put in a baseball-card shop to give me something to do when I'm not tinkering on antique cars here at the garage or overseeing my cattle out on the farm."

"Baseball-card shop?" she mumbled. "Tinkering? Overseeing cattle? When did you decide all this?"

"Last night, as a matter of fact." He reached for her, but she eluded him, backing up against the wall. Smiling, he trapped her there, his big body blocking her escape. "No promises. No commitments. Not yet. But I know one thing for sure. I don't want to lose you, Sheila. I need you. And I've never needed another woman. Not ever."

Please, don't do this to me, she wanted to beg him. *Don't say these things. Don't offer me hope. Don't let me believe that there's a chance for us. For you and me and Danny.*

She couldn't think. Couldn't breathe. Caleb was too close. Shutting her eyes to avoid the sight of him, she leaned her head back into the wall and clenched her teeth.

He caressed her cheek with his, his breath warm against her skin.

"Any chance you can close the garage for an hour?" he whispered seductively. "I've missed you a hell of a lot, sweetheart." His big, hard body pressed into hers, showing her just how much he had missed her, how very much he wanted her.

Opening her eyes, she stared at him. "Are you staying in Crooked Oak because of me?"

"Weren't you listening?" He rubbed her nose with his. "You're the only reason I'm staying. I'm not ready to give up what I've found with you. I want to hang around and see what happens."

"What—what do you think will happen?" She wanted to touch him, to open her arms and welcome him home. But her instincts warned her to go slow, to be cautious.

"I don't know," he said. "Anything. Everything."

"Or nothing."

"Something has already happened." He cupped her face in his big hands. "I've finally found a woman I need as much as I want."

"Caleb, I can't afford to play games. I have a life here. A job. And most important, I have a child who depends totally on me."

"I'm not asking you to give up any of that." Lowering

his head, he brushed her lips with his. "I just want to be a part of your life. I want us to be friends and lovers."

"What about Danny?" she asked breathlessly.

"What about Danny? Well, I think Danny and I could be buddies. I'd make sure he understood that you and I didn't know exactly where our relationship was going and that there was a good chance that I'd eventually move to Greenville."

"Substitute father for a year." Would that be fair to Danny? Somehow she'd find a way to survive when Caleb left again, but did she dare risk letting Caleb break her son's heart, too?

"Can't we take things one day at a time?"

The phone rang. Sheila jumped. Caleb glanced over his shoulder at the telephone on the wall.

"I need to answer that," she told him.

He stepped back, allowing her room to maneuver around him. She hurried across the garage and lifted the receiver from the hook.

"Hanley Garage and Tow Truck Service." Sheila paused to listen. "Oh, my God! Yes, I'll be right there."

"What's wrong?" Caleb asked. "It's not Danny, is it?"

"No. No. That was Lowell. He's on his way to an accident. There's been a bad wreck out on Highway 20. They'll need a tow truck."

"Someone you know?"

"Lowell said he was told it was Jeb and Renee Holder's teenage daughter, Misty, and a friend of hers. The girls took a turn out near the Mackays' farm doing what Mr. Mackay said was at least seventy-five miles an hour. Misty lost control of her dad's old truck."

"Then it's bad."

"Yeah, it is. I've got to go. Lowell said that Misty is trapped in the truck," she told Caleb. "We really need to talk more later. Come by the house tonight and—"

"I'll ride out to the sight of the wreck with you," he said.

"But there's no need for you to… Oh, well, okay. Let's go!"

Within ten minutes, they arrived at the scene. Lowell Redman met them the minute Sheila parked the tow truck.

"An ambulance is on its way and a med flight from Nashville, too, just in case." He explained, "Paula Carlow was thrown through the windshield. Richard, my deputy, gave her CPR and she's breathing on her own, but it looks bad. And Misty is trapped inside the truck. I'm afraid that old pile of scrap metal could catch fire any minute now."

"Then we don't have any time to waste," Sheila said. "We'll use my Jaws of Life and open that old truck like a sardine can."

"What can I do to help?" Caleb asked.

"Keep a lookout for the ambulance," Lowell said. "And if any cars stop to sightsee, tell them the sheriff said to keep going. I don't want the road blocked or a bunch of curious townsfolk getting in the way."

Caleb nodded agreement, then stood back and watched as Lowell and Sheila went to work trying to free the trapped teenager. He glanced over to an oak tree where the deputy tended to a dark-haired young girl, her face and body covered in blood. A shudder racked Caleb's body. Memories flashed through his mind. Another accident. The sight of blood. The smell of death.

No! Don't think about it! Don't remember! When he'd first awakened in the hospital nearly a year ago, he hadn't been able to remember anything at first. But day by day, the memories had returned. Vivid. Traumatic. Frightening. And then he'd wished that the temporary amnesia had lasted forever.

The wail of the ambulance brought him out of his painful thoughts. He motioned the driver onto the gravel road near the wrecked truck. The attendants jumped out and rushed over to the girl named Paula. When Lowell Redman shouted that they had the truck open, Caleb hurried toward them.

"We've got to lift her out of there. Now! Smell the gasoline?"

Lowell dove inside the truck. "Call those paramedics over here. I don't want to move her, but I don't think I have a choice."

Caleb called out and one of the medics nodded and came running to them. Working as quickly and carefully as possible, they placed a brace around her neck and then removed her from the wrecked vehicle.

Within minutes, an explosion rocked the ground and a thundercloud of fire and smoke rose into the sky.

Caleb breathed in the scent of smoke and gasoline, absorbed the disaster with all his senses. As the clear blue sky turned black with billows of smoke, he stood in the open field and trembled from head to toe.

It had all happened so fast. One minute they'd been laughing and talking and the next minute their boat had collided with another. Earlier in the day, he'd tried to persuade Wes to let him take over the helm, since his friend and teammate had been drinking heavily. But Wes had adamantly refused. The boat was his, he'd said. And he wasn't drunk!

Wes had died instantly. Kimberly had lived a few hours. The occupants of the other boat, a couple in their mid-fifties, had been killed. Wes's girlfriend, Maddie, had survived, but would always walk with a severe limp. And Caleb had lived. Lived with a useless right arm.

The fire department arrived on the scene shortly after the ambulance and set to work putting out the fire. Once the two young girls were on their way to Marshallton City Hospital, Sheila hooked up the hull of the burned vehicle and pulled the tow truck out of the field and onto the highway. That was when she noticed Caleb standing in the middle of the field. Instinctively, she knew something was wrong. Terribly wrong.

She jumped out of the truck and ran across the pasture. "Caleb? Caleb!"

He didn't respond.

When she approached him, she realized he was coated in sweat and trembling as if in the throes of a fever. Oh, my God! What was wrong with him?

Reaching out, she grabbed his shoulders and shook him soundly. He stared at her with sightless eyes. She shook him again. Harder.

"Caleb! Snap out of it!"

"They all died. Everyone except Maddie and me."

"What are you talking—" Realization dawned. "You're remembering the boating accident, aren't you? The fire and…" She wrapped her arms around him and pulled him into her embrace. "Caleb, that happened nearly a year ago. You're all right now."

"I'll never be all right," he said, his voice quivering. "Why didn't Maddie and I die, too? I've wondered a thousand times why we lived."

Sheila slipped her arm around Caleb's waist and nudged him forward, prompting him to walk. She led him out of the field and to the tow truck. He hesitated, then when she opened the passenger door, he got inside and waited like a helpless child.

When she realized he was still dazed, Sheila reached over and fastened his safety harness. She removed a clean rag from her pocket and gently wiped the perspiration from his face.

On the drive into the garage, she glanced over at him from time to time. Neither of them spoke. She had no idea what to say to him, how to comfort him. Sometimes a person had to face their demons alone.

When they arrived at the garage, she opened the passenger door. "Go on inside and wait for me in my office."

He nodded agreement and followed her instructions. She took her time unloading the hull of Holder's old truck, all the while wondering how Caleb was doing. She had to think of a way to help him, but she was afraid anything she said or did might simply make matters worse. Obviously, his viewing the wreckage and the fire had brought back bitter memories, forcing him to relive the day of the boating accident—the day his whole world had been destroyed. He had lost his lover and his career that one fateful day. And nothing would ever bring back either of them.

Sheila headed into the garage, but stopped abruptly when she caught sight of her reflection in the window. The afternoon sunshine beamed through the glass storefront of the old building. Good God, she looked awful. Her hair windblown. Her face streaked with sweat and soot. She glanced down at her overalls and saw smears of grease on the bib and dirt stains on the knees.

What difference did it make how she looked? Caleb would hardly notice her appearance. What he needed was her concern and loving care and she could give that to him without being picture perfect.

Sheila found him in the office, sitting in her swivel chair, his head resting on her desk. She laid her hand on his tense shoulder. He turned and buried his face against her bosom. Wrapping her arms around him, she whispered soothing words.

"It's all right, Caleb. I'm here."

He lifted his left arm, encircled her waist and clung to her. She caressed his soft black hair, threading her fingers through the silken strands. For what seemed like an eternity, she stood there consoling him with her touch. Vehicles passed by on the street outside. Church bells announced the time. Three o'clock. A distant train whistle blew. And somewhere in a nearby tree, springtime birds chirped.

"Do you want to talk about it?" Sheila asked.

"God, no!" As he stood slowly, he eased his arm up and around her shoulders. "I don't even want to think about it, but I can't make my brain close off the memories."

"The wreck and the fire brought it all back to you, didn't they?"

She focused her gaze on his face, studying his expressions. The pained look that narrowed his eyes told her exactly how he felt.

He took her hands in his and brought her down into his lap as he sat once again. "The whole damn thing was my fault. Kim didn't want to go with Wes and Maddie that day, but I insisted. If I'd just listened to her, she'd be alive and I'd…I'd still be pitching for the Braves."

"You had no way of knowing how that day would end. You can't blame yourself."

"I can and do blame myself," he said. "I knew Wes was drinking too much. I even tried to talk him into letting me take over as skipper, but he wouldn't hear of it. If only I'd given him no choice. I should have knocked him on his butt and taken over. Four people would be alive today if I'd done the right thing instead of the easy thing."

"Caleb, you mustn't—"

He grabbed her face in his left hand, cradling her chin in the curve between his thumb and forefinger. "But that's what I'm known for, isn't it? Doing the easy thing. That's how I've always dealt with life's problems—just do whatever's easiest, whatever causes me the least trouble."

"Don't do this to yourself." She covered his hand with hers. "The boating accident wasn't your fault. You are not responsible for those four deaths."

"Oh, I'm responsible, all right." He ran his thumb across her bottom lip. "Just like I was responsible for breaking your heart twelve years ago. I knew you were in love with me. I took your love and your innocence and then walked off and left you. I took the easy way out. I went away to college and never came back. And not once did I even bother to call and… I could have at least called you."

"Let it go, Caleb," she told him. "Let it all go. The pain. The guilt. The regrets. And the fear. You can never change the past, so lay it to rest. All you have is now. Today. This very minute."

"I loved Kim," Caleb said. "As much as the great Caleb

Bishop was capable of loving someone. But we both knew it wouldn't last. None of my relationships lasted. I was too selfish. Too self-centered. And the crazy thing was that I always chose women who were just as selfish and self-centered."

Sheila didn't want to hear this—about how much he had loved Kimberly. But if it would help Caleb to talk about the woman, then she would listen.

"How the hell can a woman like you actually care about a man like me?" He rubbed his thumb over her lips. "You're too good for me, honey. You always were."

She kissed his hand, then lifted it from her face and pressed her lips against his. She whispered into his mouth, "I love you. I've always loved you."

"I don't deserve your love," he said. "But, God help me, I want it. And I need it!"

He stared into her eyes and saw the depth of her emotions, the strength of her love, and in that one sweet moment he prayed he could be worthy of this incredible woman. She was so much more than he deserved, like a gift from on high.

While she gazed lovingly into his eyes, he took her mouth in a possessive kiss that told her more than words ever could just how much his body longed for hers. She responded greedily, taking all that he gave and returning in kind. All the hurt and anger of the past week melted inside her like winter snow beneath a springtime sun. She was powerless to resist his desperate need for her, powerless to deny the love she felt for him. She had been a fool to think she had any choice but to give herself to Caleb. She was his, had always been his. And would be his forever.

Nine

Caleb eased Sheila off his lap and onto her feet, then nudged her backward until her hips encountered the edge of the desk. "Wait here," he said, his voice low and seductive.

While she watched, her breath caught in her throat, he locked the door, closed the miniblinds and turned on the answering machine. He paused by the CD player, flipped through the assortment of discs, chose one and placed it on the deck. The slow, mournful beat of "Since I Met You Baby" filled the office. The prophetic words wove a spell around Sheila's heart. Instinctively she knew Caleb was using the old song to speak the words he couldn't say, to make the promise he wasn't able to verbalize.

As the vocalist sang of pleasing his lover, Sheila's senses heightened and anticipation raced through her veins. Caleb came toward her, taking his time. His deliberate, leisurely pace taunted her, increasing the longing within her.

"You're like a healing salve to my wounds, honey." He

stood directly in front of her, but didn't touch her. "You have a way of making me happy, when I thought I'd never be happy again."

She spread the palms of her hands out on his chest and felt the strong, urgent beat of his heart. Using his knee, he separated her thighs and eased between them. She lifted her hands to his shoulders, then circled his neck and urged his head down toward hers.

"I'm so hungry for you." He moaned the words against her lips. "I'd like to make love to you for hours. I don't want to rush, but—"

She kissed him, hard and hot and wet, thrusting her tongue into his mouth. He responded immediately, returning the demanding pressure. As the kiss deepened and intensified, robbing them both of their breaths, he sought the lapels of her overalls. Releasing the catches, he eased the straps down, pulling the garment to her waist. He hastily undid the buttons of her blouse, unhooked the front snap on her bra and exposed her breasts. While she clung to him, devouring him, he unbuttoned his own shirt and then pressed his bare chest against her breasts. Her tight nipples jabbed through his chest hair and into his warm skin.

Reaching down, he pulled off her shoes, then he lifted her up from the desk, just enough so that they could whip off her overalls. Caleb jerked the denim garment, along with her cotton panties, over her ankles and feet and tossed them to the floor. While he sucked one breast and fondled the other, she worked with the zipper on his pants. Excitement coursed through her. She slipped her hand inside his briefs and circled his swollen sex. He pulled her to the edge of the desk and plunged savagely into her. She gasped as pure sensation sang through her body. He moved with powerful, possessive jabs, creating a pounding rhythm that soon brought them both to the edge of fulfillment. The moment she cried out, her release claiming her, he completely lost control. His climax stormed through his body like a hurricane.

Holding her close, he covered her face with kisses, telling her how beautiful she was, how wonderful she was, how fabulous she made him feel.

And all the while she whispered over and over again, "I love you. I love you."

Caleb parked his Porsche behind Old Man Pickens's field and searched the group of boys huddled together for a glimpse of Danny Vance. He'd told Sheila he wanted to pick up her son from Little League practice and talk to him about *the situation. The situation* being Caleb and Sheila's relationship. He could hardly tell an eleven-year-old, "Hey, kid, I've got the hots for your mama and she feels the same way about me, so we're going to be making love every chance we get."

What he was going to have to do was find a way to protect Danny from the uncertainties of his relationship with them. He liked Sheila's son a great deal. He truly wanted to be the boy's friend. But he couldn't promise to be a father to him, at least not on a permanent basis. So, he'd just have to walk a tightrope, balancing the negative aspects and the positive, hoping all the while that he wouldn't do anything that would topple them all over into the abyss.

Danny came running toward the Porsche. Caleb threw open the passenger door. "Hop in. I'm your ride home this evening."

"Where's Mom?" Danny asked as he slid into the seat.

"Home cooking supper for us," Caleb said. "She said something about grilling hamburgers. And we're supposed to pick up some brownies from the bakery on our way home."

Danny laid his glove in his lap, then closed the door. "When did you get back into town?"

Caleb spun out of the parking area and onto the highway. "This morning."

"We missed you," Danny said. "I think Mom got upset with you because you didn't call this past week. You should have called her, you know. I heard her crying last night."

Damn! He realized now, if he hadn't before, how truly vulnerable Sheila was to him. *I love you,* she had whispered repeatedly when she'd fallen apart in his arms.

He'd said the words to a dozen other women. Three insincere little words that he'd used as easily as he had moved from bed partner to bed partner. So, why not just say them to Sheila? She wanted to hear him profess his love the way she had proclaimed hers. But he couldn't tell Sheila he loved her. Not now. Not when, for the first time in his life, he truly understood what those words meant. Commitment. Promises. Sharing. Caring. Forever after.

"Hey, what's the matter with you?" Danny asked. "You've got a funny look on your face."

"I was just thinking about your mother," Caleb told the boy. "I explained to her why I didn't call this past week and she understands."

"Did you tell her you were sorry?"

"Yeah, something like that."

"Are you moving to Greenville?" Danny fiddled with the baseball glove in his lap. "Mom said you'd been offered a job as an assistant coach."

"I decided not to take the job," Caleb said. "As a matter of fact, I've decided to stay in Crooked Oak for at least a year."

Danny's face brightened, the left edge of his mouth curving upward when he smiled. "A year? You aren't leaving. You're staying. I'll bet Mom was happy about that. She was so sure you weren't ever coming back."

"I did that once," Caleb said, then cleared his throat when he realized how close he'd come to telling the boy that he'd once walked out on his mother. "I left Crooked

Oak, my family and my friends twelve years ago and never looked back. I guess your mom figured I'd do a repeat performance this time.''

"But you came back this time," Danny said. "Did you come back because of Mom?"

Okay, here's where the situation gets sticky, Caleb thought. His relationship with Sheila was too complicated for him to figure it out, how could he expect an eleven-year-old to understand?

"Your mother was part of the reason." *She was the whole reason, but I can't tell you that, can I? If I do, you'll expect something long-term from me—something I'm not prepared to give. Not yet. Maybe not ever.*

"What's the other reason?"

"I, uh, decided I needed more time to figure out my future," Caleb said. "So, I'm going to raise a few cattle out at the farm and restore a couple of antique cars. And I've already leased a building where I'm going to put my baseball-card shop."

"A baseball-card shop!" Danny whirled around, his eyes sparkling with excitement. "Do you mean it? A real card shop here in Crooked Oak?"

"Yeah, how about that? Do you like the idea?"

"Like it? Man, I love it!"

"Well, I was wondering how you'd like to help me set things up and—"

Danny practically jumped out of his seat; only the confines of the safety belt held him down. "*Me* help *you?* You bet. You know I collect cards and I've got every Caleb Bishop card they ever put out. I know a lot about baseball cards. Just ask me anything and I bet I know the answer. I could be a real asset to you."

Caleb grinned, glanced over at Danny and chuckled. He loved the boy's enthusiasm. For a split second Caleb's mind froze on one specific thought. There was a certain look about Danny, a definite resemblance to the Bishop boys.

God, don't go there! his mind shouted. *Don't start seeing a resemblance that doesn't exist, except in your mind! Danny isn't a Bishop. He's Daniel Vance's son, not yours.*

"You could be my assistant," Caleb said as he shook the foolish notions about Danny's paternity from his mind. He couldn't have gotten Sheila pregnant graduation night. He'd used a condom. And even if the precaution had failed, Sheila would have come to him if she'd found herself pregnant. She would have told him. Of course, she would have!

"Me, Caleb Bishop's assistant. Man, the guys are going to be so jealous!"

Caleb pulled the Porsche up in the driveway at Sheila's home, directly behind Mike Hanley's Thunderbird. He killed the motor and turned to Danny. "Your mom and I are going to be dating on a regular basis and you and I are going to be seeing a lot of each other."

"Are you asking me how I feel about you and Mom being a couple? Are you asking my permission to be my mom's boyfriend?"

"Yeah, something like that. After all, you've been the man of the house since your dad died and I thought I'd better run things by you, let you know what my intentions are."

"What are your intentions?" Danny crossed his arms over his chest and narrowed his eyes. "Are you going to marry my mom?"

There it was, Caleb thought. *The* question.

Face it head-on now, buddy boy. Be honest with the kid. "Your mother and I don't have any plans to get married. We're just going to date each other exclusively. Neither of us will be seeing anyone else. We don't know what will happen in the next year, but one thing I can promise you is that I care about your mom and you. I want us to be friends, Danny, but you've got to realize, up front, that I might not be a permanent fixture in your life. I don't want you thinking of me as a...as a father."

Danny clenched his jaw tightly. "I see." Breathing deeply, he hung his head sadly and stroked the leather glove in his hand. "Caleb, if...if my mom didn't have me...you know, if she didn't have a kid, would you be more interested in marrying her?"

"What?" Caleb studied the boy's face and understood the sincerity of his question.

"Some guys wouldn't want to be saddled with a kid who wasn't their own." Danny gazed directly into Caleb's face.

Damn! Caleb swallowed. The pleading look on Danny's face was Caleb's undoing. He reached over, gripped Danny's shoulder and said, "Oh, son, you're exactly the kind of kid I'd want. Believe me, if I were the marrying kind, I might marry your mom just so I could be your dad." It was all Caleb could do not to reach out and pull the boy into his arms. Every paternal instinct in him came to full force.

"Do you mean it?" When Caleb nodded affirmatively, Danny threw his arms around him, then pulled back shyly. "I'd love for you to be my dad. If...if you were the marrying kind."

Caleb caught a glimpse of Sheila standing on the front porch, watching and waiting. Had she seen the hug? Would she think he hadn't been honest with her son, that he had made promises he couldn't keep?

Caleb turned Danny's cap backward so that the brim covered his neck. "Come on, slugger. Looks like your mom's waiting on us."

Sheila covered the three bakery brownies that were left over from the dozen Caleb had bought. He'd made a quick trip back into town when he realized he and Danny and been too involved in conversation to remember the one thing she had asked him to provide for their backyard cookout. Twilight surrounded them there in Sheila's yard and off in the woods behind the house, the chirping crickets began their nightly tune. Caleb cleared away the stack of paper plates and cups from the picnic table and tossed them into the garbage sack Danny held open for him.

Mike Hanley draped one arm around his wife's slender shoulders and caressed her small, protruding belly. "Hey, princess. This is your old man," he said to his unborn child. "Mommy and I saw our first pictures of you today and we think you're beautiful."

Christy beamed with delight, her pregnancy obviously a joy to both her and her husband. She covered Mike's hand with her own. "Your daddy's going to spoil you rotten, you know."

"How come Uncle Mike and Aunt Christy are talking to their baby while she's still in Christy's tummy?" Danny asked. "She can't hear them, can she?"

"I don't know," Sheila replied. "But I think she can. I used to talk to you before you were born."

"Ah, jeez, Mom." Danny glanced at Caleb, checking his reaction to Sheila's comment. "What's Caleb going to think?"

"I think you're a lucky guy," Caleb said, smiling at Sheila and then focusing on Danny. "You had a mom who loved you and wanted you even before you were born."

"Did you talk to me about baseball?" Danny asked.

The four adults laughed, but Caleb saw Sheila and Mike exchange an odd look.

"Sure, I did," Sheila said. "I talked to you about all sorts of things, including baseball." When Daniel hadn't been around, she had talked to Danny about Caleb. No matter how hard she tried, she could never think of Daniel as Danny's real father. In her heart of hearts, Caleb had always been and would always be Danny's dad.

Caleb watched the loving exchange between Mike and his wife, the tenderness with which Mike touched her, the love that shone so vividly in their eyes. A twinge of something unidentifiable shuddered through Caleb. Instinctively he glanced over at Sheila. She smiled at him. Warm. Welcoming. Loving. She pulled Danny back against her and wrapped her arms around him. He leaned into her, resting his head on her chest. The same twinge hit Caleb again, but this time he recognized the emotion for what it was. Jealousy. He envied Mike and Christy their happiness. He envied Daniel Vance for having possessed this remarkable woman—for having fathered her son.

This could be mine, he told himself. *Sheila could be my wife. Danny could be my son. All I have to do is reach out and bring them into my life.*

Do you have the guts to take that kind of chance? To risk everything in the hopes of finding permanent happiness?

"Hey, Uncle Mike, did you know Caleb's going to open a baseball-card shop in town?" Danny pulled away from his mother.

"Yeah, so your mom said."

"Y'all want to go through my whole collection with me?" Danny asked, glancing first at Caleb, then at his uncle.

"I sure would," Caleb said.

"I think this is our cue to clean up out here and then go out to the storage shed and take a look at Danny's baby bed," Sheila said. "It was Mike's and mine when we were babies."

"I love the idea of our little girl sleeping in her daddy's baby bed," Christy said as she picked up the leftover food items from the picnic table.

"Let's go to my room." Danny motioned to his uncle and Caleb.

"You go ahead," Mike told his nephew. "Caleb and I will be along in a few minutes. I need to talk to him about the Firebird we're keeping down at the garage for him."

"Okay, but don't be long," Danny said. "I'll lay everything out on my bed."

Mike waited until Sheila and Christy went into the house, then nodded toward the quiet road in front of Sheila's house. "Let's walk off some of that supper."

Caleb fell into step beside Mike and the two men walked a good ways before Mike spoke again.

"I'm fixing to butt into my sister's business," Mike said. "I love her and Danny a great deal and I don't want to see either of them get hurt. I figure that gives me a right to issue you a warning."

"Yeah, I suppose it does," Caleb agreed. "Go right ahead."

Mike slowed to a standstill, turned and faced Caleb, who looked him square in the eye.

"You've got to know that Sheila's in love with you," Mike said. "She always has been. She's not the kind of woman who has affairs. You and Dan Vance have been the only two men in her life."

"I know that I hurt Sheila twelve years ago when I left town and didn't ever get in touch with her again. She and I have talked about it, and I think she's forgiven me."

Mike huffed loudly. "Hell, man, that's just the problem. She'd forgive you for anything. Don't you see, she's opened herself up to you again? She's more in love with you now than ever. And she's risking her future happiness and Danny's on the chance that you'll come through for her this time. What I want to know is, are you a sure thing or a bad risk? So help me, God, if you hurt her, I'll—"

"I'm not a sure thing," Caleb admitted. "But maybe I'm not such a bad risk, either. I care about Sheila. I've never felt about another woman the way I do her. And I've been totally honest with her."

"She survived your walking out on her once before—just barely. Thanks to Dan Vance." Mike slapped his fist into the palm of his other hand. "What if you knew for sure that some guy was going to break Tallie's heart? What would you do?''

"I'd probably break his damn neck first," Caleb said. "Believe me, Mike, I understand how you feel. And I don't blame you for warning me not to hurt Sheila. That's the last thing I want to do."

"You could have stayed away."

"I could have." Caleb took a few steps, then Mike followed.

"Maybe I'm a selfish bastard, but I like what I've found with Sheila and I'm not willing to give that up."

"Not yet," Mike said. "Not until the new wears off. Not until you've worked her out of your system."

"You really don't think much of me, do you?"

"Prove to me that I'm wrong." Mike turned and headed back toward his sister's house.

Increasing his pace, Caleb went in the opposite direction. Everything Mike had said to him was true. All of his doubts were reasonable. Caleb's track record with women was dismal. Not once in his self-centered life had he ever put someone else's needs before his own. Was he doing that again? Asking Sheila to compromise her values, to accept their relationship on his terms, to risk her future and Danny's on a man who didn't know how to make a personal commitment?

Sheila loaded the washing machine, added detergent and fabric softener, then set the timer. Just as she closed the lid, Caleb walked into the kitchen.

"Is he asleep?" she asked.

"Finally," Caleb said.

"He was too excited to settle down, I guess. The thought of helping you at your card shop has him beside himself. It's hours past his bedtime. He'll probably fall asleep at school tomorrow."

"So, do you think I'm being a bad influence on him?"

Caleb came over, took the wicker laundry basket out of her hands and set it on top of the dryer.

"No. Not really. You're just not accustomed to following rules and regulations set up for an eleven-year-old. Boys Danny's age need consistency in their lives."

When Sheila turned to go to the back porch, Caleb wrapped his arms around her and pulled her back up against his chest. "Mike *talked* to me tonight when we took our walk."

"I figured that was what was going on." She snuggled into Caleb when he leaned his head over to rub his cheek against hers.

"Your big brother issued me a warning."

A shudder racked Sheila's body. "What did he say?" Mike wouldn't have said anything to Caleb about Danny's paternity. She trusted her brother. He understood that if and when the time came to tell Caleb that he was Danny's father, she would be the one to tell him.

"Mike's concerned that I'm going to hurt you, that I'm using you because I'm bored, and that when I get tired of you, I'll walk out on you again."

Sheila pivoted in his arms, turning quickly to face Caleb. "Mike had no right to say those things to you."

"Honey, Mike has every right," Caleb said. "If Tallie were getting involved with a guy like me, I'd issue him a few warnings."

"You would?"

"Damn right, I would! I'd tell him that if he broke my little sister's heart I'd rip him from limb to limb." Caleb caressed her cheek. "Don't let me break your heart. Don't let me—"

Her kiss silenced him. She didn't want to think about the possibility that she could lose Caleb again. That once the year ended, he'd leave town—leave her. She wanted to enjoy the moment—enjoy the days and weeks they could share. Surely, if there was any justice in this world, Caleb would discover that his place was here with Danny and her. Surely, he couldn't walk away and never look back—not this time. Not after all they'd shared.

Deepening the kiss, he ran his hands over her body, familiarizing himself with the feel of her breasts and her hips. She clung to him, responding eagerly, her mouth hot and wet, her fingers biting into his muscular shoulders.

And then suddenly, she shoved him away. Her breathing ragged, her face flushed, she shook her head.

"We can't."

"Why can't we?" he asked, moving toward her.

"Danny," she told him. "We can't mess around here in the kitchen. Danny could wake up and—"

Caleb pressed his index finger over her lips. "Danny is out for the night, honey. But if you don't want to take a chance, then come with me."

She resisted at first, but when he grabbed her hand and led her out onto the dark back porch, she gave herself over to him. He backed her into a pitch-black corner, a nearby oak tree blocking out the moonlight. She could see only his outline, tall, broad-shouldered and closing in on her fast. Lowering his head, he drew the tip of one breast into his mouth and sucked her greedily through the thin layer of cotton dress and bra. She quivered from head to toe. He slid his hand under her dress, lifting it, and then ran his palm up her thigh to the apex between her legs. He covered her mound with his hand and conquered her mouth with his marauding lips.

She moaned his name into his mouth when he slipped his fingers inside her panties. He eased the cotton underwear down over her hips. When they fell to her ankles, she stepped out of them. He unzipped his pants, freed his sex and bent his knees just enough to seek the entrance to her body.

Standing on tiptoe, Sheila spread her legs and braced her back against the porch column. Caleb thrust up and into her, taking her completely. She bit her lip trying not to scream with the pleasure of having him buried deep inside her. He was so big. So hard. So hot. And he filled her completely. Being possessed by Caleb was like nothing she had ever experienced. For this kind of happiness, she was willing to take a chance that it might not last forever. But her heart told her that what she felt, Caleb felt. That it couldn't be this incredible for her and not be just as perfect for him.

He slowed the rhythm, stimulating her core with each deliberate stroke of his sex. He brought her closer and closer to fulfillment as he made passionate love to her there in the dark, with only the pale moon and the twinkling stars as witnesses.

They came together in a hot, wild frenzy. Kissing. Clinging. Skyrockets of release exploding inside them. And later, much later, when they had regained their composure, Caleb zipped his slacks and picked up her panties.

"I don't suppose you'd let me move in here with you, would you?" He whispered the question in the darkness, his big hands moving caressingly up and down her arms.

"Oh, Caleb. I can't let you move in with me."

"Because of Danny?"

"This is a small town. People will talk. I don't want Danny to be ashamed because of what folks are saying about his mother."

"Then I guess we're going to have to be inventive," Caleb said. "Because I'm planning on making love to you at least once every day."

Ten

"Come on in," Susan greeted Sheila, then stepped aside to allow her friend entrance into her home. "Lunch is ready. I stopped by Pete's and picked up loaded potatoes and lemon icebox pie."

Sheila entered the homey living room, filled with a mixture of antiques Susan had inherited from her aunt and a collection of nice reproductions. "Since our talk is going to be super-serious, I suppose treating ourselves to lemon icebox pie is appropriate. You know those calories go straight to our hips."

Susan smiled weakly. "I've fixed the kitchen table for us." She led the way down the hall and into her large, warm, comfortable kitchen. "I can't believe how nervous I am just at the idea of talking to you about it."

"Is everything ready for lunch or do you want me to do anything?" Sheila asked.

"No, everything's done. Just sit. I've made fresh coffee and... Can you believe this? You and I are both going to have to make the biggest decisions of our lives sitting here at my kitchen table.''

Sheila reached out and took Susan's hands in hers. "Listen, old friend, we're going to be all right. Both of us. I already know what I have to do and I think you do, too. It's just a matter of getting some reinforcement, some support from each other. Right?''

"Yes. Maybe. I don't know. It's what Lowell wants, but I'm not sure I can actually go through with it. If he knew how I felt about—'' Susan turned around, clasped her trembling hands together and took a deep breath. Then, with her hands steadier, she poured two cups of coffee and set them on the gingham placemats on the round oak table.

Sheila sat in the oak carved-back chair. "I just love Pete's loaded potatoes. All that butter and sour cream and cheese and bacon bits.''

Susan sat across from Sheila. "So, who's going to go first, you or me?''

"We could eat and then—''

"You go first. Please.''

Sheila hated seeing Susan—highly organized, strong-willed and always-determined Susan—coming apart at the seams this way. It was so unlike her friend to let anything get the best of her. Probably the result of having been raised by a no-nonsense, old-maid aunt, Sheila surmised.

Susan's dilemma made Sheila conscious of the fact that everyone had problems, many seemingly insurmountable. But all problems had resolutions, if not solutions. The decisions they made today would affect the rest of their lives and the lives of their children.

"Okay, I'll go first,'' Sheila said. "I've made my decision, now all I have to do is work up the courage to follow through and face Caleb with the truth.''

"I think you may be worrying about nothing,'' Susan said. "After all, look how crazy Caleb is about Danny. In the past few months they've become inseparable. They're already like a father and son.''

''I know. I know. And that's one of the reasons I can't go on lying to Caleb or to Danny.'' Sheila lifted her fork and jabbed the potato, mixing the toppings together with the hot vegetable beneath. ''Over the summer, the three of us have become a family. The only way we could be closer was if Caleb actually lived in the house with us.''

''He seems happy with his life here in Crooked Oak, doesn't he? I mean, you think he's going to ask you to marry him, don't you?'' Susan sprinkled salt over her potato.

''I think he's considering it.'' Caleb had come very close, more than once, in the past few weeks to discussing marriage. With each day, each week, each month they spent together, she fell deeper and deeper in love with him, and even though he hadn't professed his love for her, she knew how much he cared. He showed her with his actions. Each kiss, each touch, each passionate encounter. And with each kind, considerate act he performed for her and for Danny. The selfish boy she remembered was gone—replaced by a caring, giving man, who worked hard at pleasing her.

I want to make you as happy as you make me, he'd told her recently.

''What are you so worried about?'' Susan asked. ''Do you honestly think Caleb won't be delighted that Danny is his son?''

''No, I think he'll be thrilled that Danny is his. But I also think he's going to hate me for lying to him, for keeping Danny's paternity a secret.'' Sheila rubbed the tips of her fingers over the smooth tabletop. ''I'm afraid of what Caleb might do, of how the truth will affect our relationship. And Danny! How's this going to affect him? He loved Daniel. How will he react to finding out that Caleb is his real father?''

''You could always keep the truth to yourself and let

Danny and Caleb just be friends and maybe even stepfather and stepson. You'll be taking a major risk with all your futures by telling them the truth."

Sheila sighed. "It was all so simple before Caleb came back to Crooked Oak. I thought he and Danny would never meet. I made sure Danny wasn't at Mr. Bishop's funeral and I kept him and Caleb apart at Tallie's wedding. But now, things are different. Caleb is a big part of our lives and if...if he doesn't ask me to marry him—"

"He can't blame you for not telling him." Susan lifted her cup and sipped on the hot coffee. "You married Dan and kept Danny's paternity a secret to protect Caleb—to give him his big chance at playing college baseball. He should thank you for making such an enormous sacrifice for him. If you'd told him about your pregnancy and he'd married you, then he'd have had to drop out of college, to find a job and support you and your baby. He'd never have become Mr. Superstar."

"I hope he sees it that way," Sheila said. "After I tell Caleb, I want us to tell Danny together."

"When are you going to tell Caleb?"

"This afternoon. I've asked him to come to my office at the garage." Sheila patted her curled fingers against her puckered lips as she huffed loudly. "I want Mike close by, just in case."

"Just in case of what?"

"In case I fall to pieces. In case Caleb decides to kill me. In case I try to chicken out at the last minute."

"Will you call me and let me know how things go?" Susan reached across the table, offering her hand to Sheila.

Sheila grabbed Susan's hand and squeezed tightly, then let go. "I promise that I'll call. Say a prayer for me. Okay?"

"I'll pray for you and you pray for me."

"That's a deal."

"Let's eat lunch before... I—I need some nourishment before I spill my guts."

They ate in relative silence, both women picking at their food, until Susan placed the pie in front of them. They devoured the rich, sweet, lemony dessert.

"It's your turn," Sheila said. "Remember that confession is good for the soul."

"Oh, God, I do feel like this is a confession!"

"No one else is ever going to know," Sheila said. "Just you and Lowell, the doctors and me. And God, of course."

"Hank will know."

"Hank may not agree to do it. He may turn Lowell down."

"What if he doesn't? What if Lowell can't convince him to...to donate his sperm and... We could adopt. I told Lowell that I don't mind waiting a few years and I don't mind adopting an older child. But he insists this way is better. This way the child will be ours. At least mine. And we'll get to share in the pregnancy and the birth and..."

"How would you feel about artificial insemination if Lowell agreed to an anonymous donor?"

"I'm not sure, but I don't think I'd have as many doubts." Susan stood and hurriedly cleared the table. "But Lowell doesn't want to use an anonymous donor. Ever since the doctors told us that Lowell is sterile, we've tried everything to correct the problem. They don't think there's any hope. Once he accepted the fact that he couldn't ever get me pregnant, the only alternative he's even considered is asking Hank Bishop to donate his sperm for an artificial insemination."

"What makes him think Hank would agree to such a plan?"

"Lowell says that he and Hank would do anything for each other, that if it were the other way around, he'd do it for Hank."

Sheila helped Susan load the dishwasher. She placed her

hand on her friend's shoulder. "It's rather ironic, isn't it? If you agree, and then Hank agrees to Lowell's plan, your child will belong to the man you've always secretly loved."

Susan jerked away from Sheila. Tears welled up in her eyes. "I'm not secretly in love with Hank Bishop! Besides, the child would belong to Lowell. Not Hank. I could never allow myself to think of the baby as Hank's. It would be so unfair to Lowell."

"You know how I felt about your marrying Lowell, but I tried not to interfere. After all, I married a man I didn't love for my own selfish reasons, so how could I try to talk you out of marrying Hank's best friend?"

"No one could have talked me out of marrying Lowell," Susan said. "I was past thirty and ready to get married and start a family. I had a teenage crush on Hank Bishop and that's all there was to it. He never even knew I existed. Oh, maybe he noticed me once or twice when I was with you and Tallie, but that was it. I bet he doesn't even remember my name, and he thinks of me only as Lowell's wife."

"So, what are you going to do?" Sheila asked.

"I'm going to make my husband happy," Susan said. "I owe Lowell so much. He's such a dear, kind man and—"

"And you feel guilty because you aren't madly in love with him, when it's so obvious to everyone that he's crazy about you."

"You know me too well."

"If you do this, can you live with the consequences? I know what it's like to look at a child every day and see his father in him. I know the heartache of keeping the truth a secret."

"It's what Lowell wants."

"But is it what you want?"

"Yes. Heaven help me, yes, it's what I want!"

Sheila wrapped her arms around Susan and held her while she cried.

* * *

Caleb locked the door on his Main Street card shop,
laced two fingers through his key ring and whistled as he
walked down the sidewalk toward his car. The day was
gloomy and overcast, with gray clouds swirling around in
the sky. It was only early September and already autumn
was sending out feelers.

The day might look rainy, but Caleb's spirits were bright
and sunny. Nothing—absolutely nothing—could bring him
down off the emotional high he was on.

He slid behind the wheel of the Porsche, then checked
his jacket pocket to make sure the little velvet box was still
there. He hadn't planned on seeing Sheila until tonight—
he'd even made plans to take her into Nashville for the
evening. But she'd called him a couple of hours ago and
asked him to meet her at the garage this afternoon.

"We need to talk," she'd said. "I have something very
important to tell you."

Her voice had sounded oddly strained and even sad, but
whatever was bothering her wouldn't amount to a hill of
beans once he popped the big question. No matter what
was worrying her, she'd forget it in a minute once he asked
her to be his wife.

The realization that he wanted to spend the rest of his
life with Sheila Vance had come to him slowly during the
past few months.

With each passing day, time with her became more precious to him—so precious that the thought of a future without her scared the hell out of him. Sometime when he
hadn't been watching, Sheila's sweetness and honesty and
genuine love had possessed him completely.

No matter where he went or what he did in the years
ahead, he knew one thing for sure and certain—he wanted
Sheila and Danny with him.

Caleb removed the tiny box from his pocket, flipped
open the lid and gazed at the ruby and diamond ring. A
large marquise-cut ruby glistened like rose-red fire in the

center of a circle of small diamonds. He'd bought the ring and made plans for their evening when he'd made a secret trip to Nashville two days ago. He wanted this evening to be perfect. A night Sheila would never forget.

Strange how the right woman could change a man's whole life, he thought as he closed the lid and returned the box to his pocket. He'd never thought of himself as a husband and a father. Not until Sheila and Danny had opened his eyes to the truth—true happiness came from loving and being loved.

He was one lucky SOB to have found a woman like Sheila. And Danny was a bonus. A son who practically worshiped the ground he walked on. Life was good. Better than he'd ever thought it could be after the boating accident.

When his career ended, he thought he'd lost everything. He'd been wrong. He might never be a star athlete again, but as long as he had Sheila and Danny, he'd never be lonely or unhappy.

"I want to be alone with Caleb," Sheila said. "But I need you close by. I don't know if I have the courage to go through with this, but if I do tell him the truth, I have no idea how Caleb will react."

"You're doing the right thing," Mike told her. "You should have done this years ago."

"Don't scold me now. Don't tell me what I should have done and why I should have done it. Finally being honest with Caleb is hard enough without playing what-if games."

Mike gave his sister a reassuring hug. "It's going to be okay. Trust me. No matter how Caleb reacts initially, you'll find a way to make him understand that what you did, you did for him."

"Did I, Mike? Was I really trying to protect Caleb's dream of a career by not burdening him with a wife and child, or was I protecting myself from the chance Caleb would reject me and my baby?''

''Now who's playing the what-if game?''

Sheila had told herself for the past twelve years that she had kept Danny's paternity a secret in the beginning for Caleb's sake, so that he didn't have to give up his dreams. And to a certain extent, that was true. But in those quiet, dark moments of total honesty, she had admitted to herself that she had been afraid that if she had confronted Caleb with the truth, he might have chosen baseball over her and their baby. Now, neither she nor Caleb would ever know what choices he would have made.

Glancing out the window, Sheila saw Caleb park the Porsche and open the driver's door. ''He's here,'' she told Mike.

''I'll speak to Caleb on the way out, then I'll lock the front door and put up the Out To Lunch sign. That should give you two all the privacy you need.''

''Stay close, okay? My instincts tell me that when this is over, I'm going to need my big brother to lean on.''

He tapped beneath her chin with his index finger. ''Maybe we've both underestimated Caleb Bishop. I guess we'll find out today just what he's made of.''

Mike nodded and said hello to Caleb on his way out of the office.

Sheila stood, smoothed the pleats in her black slacks and laced her fingers together in front of her.

Caleb came over, put his arms around her and kissed her. ''Don't you look pretty this afternoon.''

''Thank you. I've been wearing a little makeup to work for the past few months and I've bought a couple of new outfits.''

''I wasn't talking about the makeup or the clothes.'' He nuzzled her neck. ''I'm talking about you.''

She smiled shyly. ''Caleb, we're going to have a very

serious talk and I don't think I can concentrate as long as you're so close."

He released her, stepped back and plopped down in her swivel chair. Grinning at her with that cocky, seductive smile, he crossed his arms over his chest. "Is that better?"

She nodded. "Much. Thanks."

"Okay. What's so urgent and so serious that it couldn't wait until tonight?" he asked. "I've made some pretty special plans for us tonight, you know."

"Caleb, we need to talk about Danny."

He stared quizzically at her. "Danny? I thought everything was fine with Danny and me. We're best buddies and—"

"You're more than best buddies."

"Are you still worrying about the fact that Danny might see me as a substitute father? Because if that's the problem, I think I have the perfect solution."

Sheila paced the floor. *Give me the strength and courage to do this. And please, let me say all the right things.*

"You can't solve the problem I have, except by listening to me and trying to understand," she said.

"Didn't you hear what I said, honey? I've got the solution to all our problems, but I want to wait until tonight and do this right. After all, I've never done this sort of thing before and—"

"Caleb, what are you talking about?" She had never known Caleb to ramble the way he was doing. What was he trying to tell her?

"I'm talking about you and me and Danny and the future and my being more to Danny than just his best buddy." Caleb ran his left hand into the inside pocket of his jacket. "But I don't want to propose to you in the garage. I want—"

"Propose to me!" Sheila felt as if all the air had been knocked out of her. Had she heard him correctly? Had he said *propose* to her?

"Yes, propose." He shot up out of the chair, grabbed her around the waist and whirled her around the room. "But I'm not going to do it here and now. I've got a romantic evening planned for us. The Finches have already agreed to let Danny spend the night with them. We're going to drop him by their house on our way to Nashville and then pick him up in the morning."

"A marriage proposal?" Sheila's mouth gaped open; she pulled away from Caleb and stared at him with wide, round eyes.

"Now that you know my secret, can't any discussion about my relationship to Danny wait for later?"

"No!" She screamed the word, her voice louder and stronger than she had intended.

"Why not? Unless you want me to go ahead and propose to you right here and now. But this won't be a very romantic memory to share with our kids and grandkids, when they ask about—"

"Caleb, will you please shut up!"

He walked over to her, knelt on one knee and clasped her hand in his. "Sheila Hanley Vance, will you be—"

She jerked her hand away. "Stand up, dammit!"

"Honey, what's wrong?" He stood, then pulled her into his arms. "Why are you crying?"

"I—I had no idea you were planning to propose to me." She spoke so softly he barely heard her.

He tilted her chin upward, then wiped away her tears with his fingertips. "If you think you're surprised, you should have been around when I realized that I wanted to spend the rest of my life with you, that—"

She covered his mouth with her hand. "No. Wait. Please, don't say any more. I have something to tell you. Something I should have told you twelve years ago."

She stepped out of his embrace and faced him boldly, despite the fear raging inside her.

He breathed deeply, exhaled, and locked his gaze with hers.

"I thought we'd put the past behind us," he said. "I thought we'd buried all those ghosts and started out with a clean slate."

"Danny was eleven years old this past March," she said. "I've been holding my breath all these months, afraid Danny would mention his birthday or that you'd ask about it."

"I don't see what Danny's birthday has to do— March? Danny was born in March?"

"Yes. Six months and two days after I married Daniel Vance."

Caleb's face paled. He balled his left hand into a tight fist.

"You were pregnant when you and Dan got married."

"Yes."

"But not pregnant with Dan's baby."

"No."

"Then Danny is...Danny is—"

"Your son."

Caleb felt as if he'd been poleaxed. The pain hit him in the gut, then spread through his body and throbbed inside his head. *Your son. Your son. Your son.*

Danny was his. God in heaven, he should have known. Every time he'd looked at the boy. Every time he'd watched him playing ball. Every time he'd caught Sheila staring oddly at the two of them together. Damn fool that he was, he'd dismissed his suspicions as ridiculous notions. He had trusted Sheila in a way he'd never trusted another soul. She was the most honest woman he'd ever known. She never would have lied to him.

"You lied to me! You let me think— What about Dan Vance? Did he know? Or did you lie to him, too?"

"Dan knew. He found me crying one day and asked what was wrong. I don't know why, but I just blurted the truth and he…he was so kind and understanding and… He offered to marry me and take care of me and my baby."

"Our baby," Caleb said. "You let another man claim my son. How could you have done that?"

"I didn't have any choice," she told him. "You didn't love me or want me or—"

"I had a right to know. I should have been the one to take care of you and Danny. I would have married you."

"Would you have? Would you really have married me and given up your chance to play college baseball? Given up your dreams to be a major league player someday? Danny and I would have ruined all your plans and destroyed all your dreams. Believe it or not, Caleb, I loved you too much to deny you the fulfillment of those dreams."

She held her hands out to him pleadingly. He glared at her. His jaw clenched.

He wanted to strangle her. Damn her for playing God with their lives! "If you loved me so much, how could you have denied me my son?"

"I honestly thought I was doing what was best for all of us. You didn't love me. Daniel Vance did. And you would have hated me and Danny if I had asked you to give up your chance to play college baseball. If you'd been saddled with a wife and child—neither of which you wanted—you'd have had to find a full-time job. We didn't have anyone who could have helped us. We were both a couple of poor kids with poor families."

Thunder rumbled through the sky. A bright flash of lightning streaked across the western horizon. Only then did Sheila realize it was raining.

Wild, crazy thoughts raced through Caleb's mind as he assimilated all the information. "Maybe you're right. I'm not saying you are, but maybe… I was a self-centered kid back then and I hadn't given you any reason to trust me."

A tiny ray of hope filled Sheila's heart like summer sunshine.

"I didn't want to ruin your life. You didn't mean to get me pregnant. You'd used a condom. You'd tried to protect me."

He stared at her, his eyes glazed with a fine mist. "Why didn't you tell me when I came back to town last spring? Why didn't you tell me the truth after you and I started dating and Danny and I became—" Caleb swallowed hard "—best buddies."

"I didn't trust you," she admitted. "I couldn't take a chance that after I told you the truth about Danny—that you are his biological father—that you would love him enough to...to—"

"What did you think? That I'd say I don't care that Danny is really my son? I don't have room in my life for a kid? You've done a great job raising him without me, so neither of you need me now? Is that it? You were so sure twelve years ago that I didn't want you or Danny that you kept him a secret from me. So why should you think things are different now? That I was different?"

"Caleb, please... I do believe you're a different kind of man now. If I didn't believe that, I never would have told you about Danny today."

Caleb raked his left hand across the top of Sheila's desk, sending papers, folders and adding machine crashing to the concrete floor. He cursed a blue streak.

Sheila stood helplessly, paralyzed with pain, and watched Caleb storm out of her office.

Danny Vance hid in the corner of the garage and peeped out the window. As he watched Caleb stomp through the rain, get in his Porsche and drive away, his thin body trembled as tears poured down his cheeks.

They hadn't known he was there, that he'd been listening, that he'd heard every word they'd said.

He was supposed to be at Peewee football practice this afternoon, but when it started lightning so bad, the coach had sent them home. Tanner's mom had dropped him by the garage.

Danny is my son! You were so sure I didn't want you or Danny. Didn't want you or Danny. Didn't want Danny. Didn't want Danny.

Caleb Bishop was his father. Not Daniel Vance. Caleb Bishop. And Caleb hadn't wanted him. His mom had been so sure that Caleb hadn't wanted him that she'd married someone else. The man he'd thought was his father wasn't.

So why should you think things are different now? That I'm different now? Caleb's angry voice reverberated loudly inside Danny's head.

Caleb still didn't love him or his mother. He still didn't want them. Damn him! Damn Caleb Bishop to hell!

Danny ran out of the garage, out into the rain and down the street. He didn't know where he was going, but he knew one thing—he never wanted to see Caleb Bishop again as long as he lived!

Eleven

Sheila checked her watch again. Where could he be? Coach Young should have dropped Danny at the garage an hour ago. At first she'd thought that perhaps Danny had gone to Caleb's shop without asking her permission. He spent so much time there, maybe he'd simply forgotten to let her know where he was going. But there was no answer at the card shop and no answer at Caleb's house. Dear God, she couldn't let Caleb tell their son the truth. She had been the one who'd kept his true paternity a secret from him; it was her right and her duty to be the one to explain why she had lied to him all his life.

"I finally got hold of Coach Young," Mike said.

"And?"

"Don't panic." Mike gripped her shoulder. "They ended Peewee practice early today because of the bad weather and he took several of the boys home himself, but not Danny. He—"

"Oh, God! Why didn't Danny call me? You don't suppose he walked from the practice field do you?"

Mike shook his head. "Coach Young said that he's sure Danny caught a ride with one of the other kids. Probably Tanner."

"Teresa Finch!" Sheila reached for the phone. "Maybe Danny went home with Tanner and Teresa just forgot to call me."

She dialed her friend's number, then waited as the phone rang. Her heartbeat accelerated. *Please, Lord, let Danny be there. Please. Please.*

"Hello?" Teresa said.

"Teresa, this is Sheila. Is Danny at your house?" She held her breath.

"Why, no, he isn't. I dropped him off at the garage nearly two hours ago. I waited until he went inside. Isn't he with you?"

"No, he isn't here and we can't find him."

"Oh, dear. Well, maybe he's with Caleb. You do know that Caleb asked us to keep Danny tonight. He said y'all would drop Danny by on your way to Nashville."

"You said that you saw Danny go inside the garage two hours ago?" Two hours ago, Caleb Bishop had walked out on her—after she'd told him that he was Danny's biological father. "Oh, God, no!"

"Sheila, what's wrong?" Teresa asked.

Mike put a supporting arm around his sister's waist. She slumped against him as her knees buckled. He eased her over into a chair and took the phone away from her.

"Teresa, this is Mike Hanley. Danny isn't here. We haven't seen him and we can't find him anywhere. We're awfully worried about him."

"It's not like Danny to run away," Teresa said. "When I let him out at the garage, he was fine. I mean, he wasn't upset or anything. He and Tanner had horsed around in the back seat all the way from the practice field."

"Look, would you do me a favor?" Mike asked. "Would you contact all of Danny's friends and find out if any of them have seen him?"

"What's going on, Mike?"

"We're afraid Danny might have accidentally overheard something that upset him," Mike said. "I can't explain right now, but…"

"Something about Caleb and Sheila? But I thought…well, when Caleb asked us to keep Danny tonight so he could take Sheila into Nashville, we…that is, I assumed—"

"Call me as soon as you've checked with the other parents."

"I will. And let us know if you find Danny."

Mike hung up the receiver, bent down on one knee and clasped Sheila's trembling hands. "Don't fall apart on me, sis. You don't know for sure Danny overheard your and Caleb's conversation."

"Why else would he have run off? Danny's never done anything to worry me. Something upset him terribly or…or—oh, Mike, what if someone abducted Danny?"

"Don't go there. Don't even think it." He squeezed her hands. "You stay here, in case Danny comes back or calls, or in case Teresa discovers him at another friend's house. I'll drive around town to find out if anybody's seen him."

"If he heard some of the things Caleb said, he…he might have misunderstood. There's no telling what Danny is thinking. Oh, Mike, what have I done?"

"You haven't done anything to hurt Danny. If he did overhear any part of your conversation with Caleb, then you'll have some explaining to do when we find him." Mike released her hands and stood. "Maybe you'd better try calling Caleb again."

"Do you think Danny would have gone to him?"

"It's possible."

Sheila nodded, hoping that Danny *was* with his father.

She'd never been so scared. If Danny wasn't with Caleb, where could he be? And what must he be thinking? About Caleb? About her? And about himself?

Caleb spun the Porsche into the driveway, splattering mud and flinging water from the puddles in the gravel road. He jumped out of the car and ran toward the house as rain drenched him to the skin.

He slammed the kitchen door behind him. Shaking his head, he created a halo of moisture around him. He shivered. It was a damn cold rain.

He'd been driving around for the past three hours—going nowhere fast. No matter how fast he drove or how far he went, he couldn't escape the truth—Danny Vance was his son, and Sheila had kept that from him for twelve years.

Caleb undressed in his bedroom, dumped his wet clothes on the bathroom floor and turned on the shower. He stepped beneath the warm water and let the spray pelt his body.

A part of him wanted to punish Sheila for keeping his child from him. And yet another part of him wanted to take her into his arms—to comfort her and tell her he understood why she'd lied to him.

He had known disappointment and pain before and he had survived, if only barely. But this was different. He had trusted Sheila as he'd never trusted anyone else. He had believed in her, in her love and goodness and honesty. If any other woman had been Danny's mother, he might have questioned the boy's paternity when he started noticing certain similarities—Bishop traits—they had in common. But he had trusted Sheila so implicitly that he had dismissed what his own gut instincts told him.

Caleb stepped out of the shower, dried off and went into the bedroom in search of dry clothes. He dressed hurriedly, haphazardly, in jeans and long-sleeved plaid shirt, then flopped down across the bed. Staring up at the ceiling, he replayed the scene in his mind. He could hear the uncertainty in Sheila's voice, could see the fear in her eyes, could sense the pain she felt.

Would you really have married me and given up your chance to play college baseball?

Would he have? God, help him, he didn't know. He couldn't be sure that he would have chosen to do the right thing twelve years ago.

I loved you too much to deny you the fulfillment of those dreams.

Caleb didn't doubt for a minute that she meant what she'd said. She had loved him. She had sacrificed a life of the three of them together for the sake of his future career. She had made what she thought was the right decision— the only decision under the circumstances.

I didn't have any choice. You didn't love me or want me or—

She was right. He hadn't loved her then—twelve years ago, when he'd gotten her pregnant. He hadn't loved anyone except himself.

You would have hated me if I'd asked you to give up your chance to play college baseball.

Was she right about that, too? Would he have hated her? Would he have resented their baby?

Caleb squeezed his eyes shut as pain shot through his temples. Flinging his arms across his forehead, he groaned. Of course, Sheila was right. She'd known him so well, known nothing had been more important to him when he was eighteen than a chance to play college ball.

So, he had to concede that her decision not to tell him that she was pregnant had been the right one—for all of them. She had protected not only herself and Danny, but she had protected him, too.

It was a wonder that she didn't hate him, that she'd been able to keep on loving him all these years.

But why the hell hadn't she been honest with him after she knew he wasn't going to skip town a second time? Why had she waited all summer to tell him that Danny was his son?

Because she didn't trust you, you big dope! She told you today because she finally trusted you, because she finally believed that you had changed, that you were a man capable of understanding and forgiveness.

And what the hell had he done? The first big test she'd given him, he'd failed miserably. He'd said some horrible things to her. He'd blamed everything on her. And he'd walked out on her in a childish fit of rage, acting like the self-centered bastard he'd always been.

Caleb sat up straight in the middle of the bed. He had to get his act together. Had to talk to Sheila. Had to work through his problems with her before they told Danny.

How would the boy react? How would Danny feel about his big hero when he knew the truth—that he was his biological father? That twelve years ago a chance at a baseball career might have meant more to him than anything—even his own child?

Oh, God, he had to find a way to make Danny understand. He wanted his son to continue admiring him and liking him, and yes, he wanted Danny to love him. He'd been afraid to admit to himself how much Danny meant to him, afraid to say that he loved the boy. And even though he'd planned to propose to Sheila, he still hadn't been prepared to tell her that he loved her.

But if he couldn't truly love Sheila and Danny, he was going to lose them. If he didn't find a way to make up for the past, the three of them never could have a future together.

Just as he reached for the phone to call Sheila, it rang. Startled, he jumped, then grabbed the receiver with a shaky hand.

"Hello?"

"Caleb, is Danny with you?" Sheila's voice trembled.

"No, he's not with me. What's wrong?"

"Danny's missing," she said, choking on her tears. "Football practice was called off because of the weather and...and Teresa Finch dropped Danny off at the garage over two hours ago. But we can't find him!"

"Over two hours ago...then he might have overheard us."

"Yes, he might have. And if he did, we have no way of knowing exactly what he heard or how he interpreted it. Oh, Caleb, I'm scared. Danny's never—"

"Where are you, at home or at the garage?"

"I'm at the garage, but Mike's fixing to take me home. He's looked all over town for Danny. Nobody's seen him."

"I'll meet you at your house," he said. "And don't worry. We'll find Danny."

Danny's feet mired up in the sludge as he made his way deeper into the woods. Tears streamed down his face, mixing with the rain that matted his hair to his head and soaked through his shirt and jeans. He wasn't sure where he was going. All he knew was that he had to get away—he didn't ever want to see Caleb Bishop again. And he didn't want to face his mother. She had lied to him. She'd told him that Daniel Vance was his father. Why had she lied to him?

Because she knew Caleb didn't want you, that's why!

Who else knew the truth? he wondered. Did Uncle Mike know? And what about Tallie and Susan and Mr. and Mrs. Finch? Did everybody in Crooked Oak know? Everybody but him? Did the other guys know? Had they been laughing behind his back all these months?

Danny's foot caught on a large tree branch that lay atop the underbrush. Losing his balance, he tumbled forward and fell, facedown, onto the ground. The ball and glove he'd been clutching dropped out of his hands. Mud went into his mouth and up his nose. For a couple of minutes the mire strangled him. He coughed and spat as he shoved himself up onto his knees. His hands sunk into the rotted leaves that covered the wet earth.

Sobs racked his slender body. He looked straight up, through the towering tree branches, at the gray evening sky. It was going to be dark soon. He couldn't stay here. If he did, they'd be sure to find him. He had to keep going, stay moving, and get as far away from Crooked Oak as he could before nightfall.

Sheila flung open the front door. Caleb grabbed her the moment he got close enough to touch her. They stood in the doorway, clinging to each other.

"Any word on Danny?" Caleb asked, easing his arm around Sheila's waist as he closed the door and led her into the living room.

"We've called everyone we know," Mike said. "I've alerted all his friends to let us know if he contacts any of them. And I've driven up and down every street in town and asked everyone in every shop. Nobody's see Danny since Teresa Finch dropped him off at the garage."

Caleb looked at Sheila. Her eyes were swollen and red. Sniffling, she gazed into his eyes. "Oh, Caleb. What if...if—"

Caleb encircled her in his embrace and stroked her back tenderly. Burying his face against her neck, he whispered, "God, honey, what did I say that might have upset him? I can't remember much of anything I said. I was so angry and hurt and... If he heard us arguing...if he misunderstood something I said...if—"

Sheila laid her hand over Caleb's mouth. "I think we can assume he heard part, if not all, of our conversation. And if he did, then he knows that you're his biological father and he knows that I've lied to you and to him his entire life."

Caleb pulled her hand away from his mouth and laced

their fingers together. "Don't blame yourself. If this is anyone's fault, it's mine."

"Caleb—"

"If I hadn't reacted the way I did when you told me, Danny wouldn't have run. God knows what he thinks of me...what you think of me." He pulled Sheila over to the sofa and brought her down beside him as he sat. He kept his arm around her and their hands clasped together.

"I think you had every right to be upset and angry," Sheila said. "I should have told you about Danny months ago."

Mike cleared his throat. Sheila and Caleb glanced at him. "My sister did what she thought was best for all of you. She sacrificed her own happiness for your sake and Danny's."

"Mike, please, don't—" Sheila tried to stop her brother from explaining.

"It's all right, honey," Caleb said. "Mike's right. I understand why you did what you did. I think I understood when you told me, but I was just so hurt and confused and so filled with guilt that I tried to blame you for everything." He cupped her face in his hands. "You did what you thought was right for all three of us—for you and Danny and for me."

"Do you really believe that?" Tears threatened to overflow from her eyes. "You can't imagine how desperately I wanted to tell you that I was pregnant with your baby, but—" She gulped, swallowing her tears. "I wanted you to have your chance. I couldn't...couldn't..."

Caleb pulled her into his arms. She laid her head on his chest and sobbed so hard that her body shook. He comforted her, telling her over and over again that she shouldn't blame herself.

When she finished weeping, Sheila sucked in deep, calming breaths and squeezed Caleb's hand tightly. "We're going to have to call Lowell."

"Yeah, honey, you're right. We need some help to search for Danny." When Sheila started to get up, Caleb restrained her. "No. You just sit here and take it easy. I'll call Lowell. I'm Danny's father and it's way past time I started acting like it."

Within an hour Lowell Redman had organized a manhunt and half the men in Crooked Oak, some with their hunting dogs, showed up at Sheila's house. Lowell and Mike and Caleb split the men into three groups and began independent searches, all starting from the garage—the last place anyone had seen Danny Vance.

Susan Redman and Teresa Finch came over to stay with Sheila and man the telephones—both had brought their cellular phones to add two extra lines. As the hours passed and evening turned to night, the rainstorm worsened. Sheila paced the floor and despite her friends' constant hovering, she felt totally alone. Nothing they said or did to comfort her alleviated any of the agony she experienced.

The front door flew open. Caleb and Bill Finch wiped their feet on the outdoor mat, then hurried into the dry warmth of the house. Sheila raced toward Caleb.

"Did you find him?"

Caleb shook his head. "No."

"Oh, God!" Sheila crumbled into Caleb's arms, falling apart as he held her. "Where is he? What's happened to him?"

Tears glazed Caleb's eyes. He bit down on his lower lip.

"Danny's all right. He has to be. And we're going to find him."

"Our group came back to dry out and get some coffee, then we'll head back out and Mike's group will come in," Bill Finch said. "We're going to keep a group of searchers out there until we find Danny."

"I want to go with you when you go back out." Sheila grabbed the lapels of Caleb's jacket.

"Honey, there's nothing you can do. I wish you'd stay

here.'' He looked into her eyes—eyes that plainly showed her suffering— and knew he couldn't deny her anything. ''All right. You'll come with me and we'll find our son together.''

''Oh, my,'' Teresa Finch cried.

''Hush up,'' Bill Finch told his wife.

''You hush up,'' Teresa said. ''I just think it's sad that Caleb and Sheila and Danny had to be apart all those years.''

Hours later Caleb took Sheila into the bathroom, stripped her drenched clothes from her body, undressed himself and then pulled her into a hot shower. After drying them both, he carried her into her bedroom, pulled her gown on over her head and put her to bed. She lay there and watched him hand his wet clothes through the door to Bill Finch.

''I'll get these in the dryer right away,'' Bill said. ''Susan's bringing in some soup and sandwiches, so you'd better put something on.''

Caleb jerked a cotton afghan off the foot of the bed, wrapped it around his hips and tied the ends in a knot. ''Tell her to come on in.''

Susan entered, carrying a large tray filled with food. She set the tray down on the cedar chest at the foot of Sheila's bed. ''You two eat something, even if you don't feel like you could eat a bite. You've got to keep your strength up.'' She hugged Sheila. ''Wherever Danny is, he's okay.''

Sheila wanted to believe her friend, wanted desperately to convince herself that her son wasn't out there hurt and scared and frightened. He was just a little boy. Only eleven years old. What if someone had found him and hurt him? What if some wild animal had attacked him? What if a poisonous snake had bitten him? What if—

She trembled with the force of the emotions ripping out her heart.

Susan hugged Sheila fiercely once again, then when

Caleb sat on the edge of the bed, Susan got up and let him take Sheila into his arms.

"See if you can't get her to eat just a little something," Susan said. "I don't think she's had a bite since we ate lunch together yesterday."

Once Susan left, Caleb nodded toward the tray. "She's right, you know. You need to eat something."

"I can't. But—but you should eat."

"Maybe later," he said.

"After we find Danny, we…" She burst into tears again.

Caleb held Sheila, allowing her to cry herself to sleep. He eased her down onto the bed, lay beside her and held her until he, too, drifted off.

At daybreak, two hours later, Caleb woke with a start. When he shot straight up in bed, Sheila awoke and cried out.

"What's wrong?"

"I don't know." Caleb trembled convulsively. "It's Danny. Don't ask me how I know, I just know."

She wrapped her arms around Caleb and laid her head on his back. "They—they've found him, haven't they?"

"Yeah, I think so…or they're about to find him. I feel it—" Caleb patted his fist against his belly "—here, in my gut."

"I know," she said. "I feel it, too."

Caleb got out of bed and realized that sometime during their nap, someone had removed the untouched food tray from the cedar chest and replaced it with his clean, dry clothes. Sheila rummaged in her closet, grabbed a shirt and overalls and then the two of them dressed hurriedly.

Someone rapped softly on the door, then Susan stuck her head in, and said, "Lowell's here. He has some news."

Together, parents united in their love and concern, Sheila and Caleb walked down the hall and into the living room where Lowell Redman and a couple of his deputies waited.

"Have y'all found him?" Sheila looked pleadingly at the sheriff.

"We found his leather glove and the ball Caleb autographed," Lowell said.

"What?" Sheila asked. "You found what?"

"After he left the garage, Danny must have come home and got his glove and the baseball," Lowell told them.

"Are you sure they're Danny's?" Caleb asked.

"Yeah, we're sure." Lowell placed his hand on Caleb's shoulder.

"We found them in Smith Woods, about half a mile from the old rock quarry. We found footprints in the mud leading all the way to the entrance to the old quarry."

"Oh, Lowell, you don't think he went in there, do you?" Sheila held her hands together in a prayerful gesture. "With all the rain we've gotten, the quarry will be full. What if he—"

Caleb grabbed her. "Don't even think it."

"The gates were locked and we didn't see any sign of Danny, but that doesn't mean he didn't find a way to get in there. He could have climbed the fence or found a hole somewhere. Some of the men were about to cut through the chain fence and check the old shed to see if Danny might have taken shelter in there for the night."

"Please, we—we have to find him." Sheila clung to Caleb. "I want to go to the quarry now. Right now."

"Come on," Caleb said, then turned to Lowell. "Are you going to drive us?"

Lowell nodded agreement, then followed Danny's parents out onto the front porch. Morning dawned, spreading her pink fingers across the eastern horizon. A cool breeze glided over the treetops. Off in the distance bloodhounds howled.

Twelve

Danny awoke when he heard the voices. Cold, hungry and scared, he huddled in the corner of the ramshackle shed near the rock quarry. He had wanted to get away from Crooked Oak last night, but it had gotten dark and when lightning had struck a tree only a couple of hundred feet away from him, he'd known he had to find a safe place to stay. Then he'd realized he was close to the old quarry. He'd heard the men in town talk about how when they'd been kids, they'd used the old quarry as a swimming hole because the enormous cavern stayed full of rainwater.

When he heard the voices drawing closer, Danny peeped out the window, through the broken panes, and saw four men searching the area. They were looking for him! His mother had probably called Lowell when she'd realized he was missing.

Danny eased open the back door. Sneaking around the opposite side of the shed, he ran toward the old swimming hole. If he could make it to the back side of the quarry, he would crawl under the loose fencing where he'd gotten in last night.

"I thought I saw something," one of the men yelled.

"Where?" another asked.

"Over yonder. Look. It's a kid, all right."

"Danny?" a man called out to him. "Danny Vance, is that you, boy?"

They'd found him! He couldn't let them catch him. He wasn't going to talk to his mother. He couldn't. Not yet. And if they caught him, they'd take him home. And his mother would probably make him talk to Caleb. He didn't want to hear anything Caleb Bishop had to say. Not now. Not ever!

"What if he did go to the old quarry? What if he fell in?" Sheila glanced over at Lowell, who sat on her left and was driving. Caleb, who sat on her right, gave her a reassuring hug.

"We don't know if he's there or not," Lowell said. "Besides, even if he got in under or over the fence, there's no reason he would have gone anywhere near the water."

"But it was dark. He might not have realized..." Sheila stopped herself before she voiced the words that would make her fears even more real. "It's just that I remember what happened to Hank when y'all were boys. I was just a little kid myself, but I recall that your saving Hank's life was all this town talked about for six months."

"It was no big deal. If I'd gotten the cramp instead of Hank, he'd have saved me from drowning." Lowell kept his gaze focused on the road ahead of him.

"You've always been too modest," Caleb said. "Hank knows he owes you his life. He's said more than once that he'd do anything for you."

"There's the quarry," Lowell said, his cheeks flushed, apparently embarrassed.

Sheila noticed that one of the deputies who stood at the entrance gates was waving at them.

Lowell pulled his car over to the side of the road and rolled down his window. "What's up, Kendrick?"

"We found him, sir," the deputy said.

"You found him!" Sheila gripped Caleb's hand. "Is he—is he—"

"He's all right, ma'am. Physically all right. He's dirty and his clothes are torn, but…well, he won't let us get anywhere near him."

"What do you mean?" Caleb asked.

"I mean, the kid is sitting on the edge of the old swimming hole and he's saying that if anybody comes near him, he's jumping in and drowning himself."

"Oh, my God!" Sheila balled both hands into tight fists. "Let me out of here. I'm going to—"

"Calm down, honey," Caleb said. "I know your first instinct is to go out there and yell at him, but you have to remember that Danny's upset and very angry. Angry at me and maybe angry at you."

"Caleb's right," Lowell said. "I'm pretty sure that if Danny did jump in, he'd swim until we pulled him out. But we all know that the quarry is dangerous and anything might happen if Danny jumps or even accidentally falls in."

"Danny's an excellent swimmer. He wouldn't drown." Sheila shoved against Caleb's shoulder. "I want to get out. Now."

Caleb opened the door, got out of the car and held open his hand to Sheila. She accepted his assistance. Lowell exited from the driver's side. The deputy spoke quietly to Lowell, then hurried toward his patrol car.

"I'm getting the rescue squad out here, just in case," Lowell said.

"You think Danny's in trouble, don't you? What are you not telling us?" Caleb asked.

"Sheila," Lowell called to her when she ran toward the gap the men had cut in the eight-foot chain-link fencing. "Danny says he doesn't want to see you or Caleb."

She glared at Lowell, her eyes filled with uncertainty. "Did he tell the deputy that he didn't want to see us?"

"He told Kendrick that you had lied to him and he didn't trust you." Lowell spoke softly, sadly, bowing his head. "He said he never wanted to see Caleb ever again. He said that he hated him. You're dealing with an emotionally distraught child and we can't rule out suicide."

Sheila gasped loudly. "Suicide! Lowell, this is Danny we're talking about, not some…some—"

"I'm going to talk to him," Caleb said. "I'm the one he hates, the one he really blames for everything."

Sheila grabbed Caleb's arm. "What are you going to say to him?"

"I'm going to tell him the truth."

"All of it?"

"Yes."

Caleb glanced over at Lowell, who nodded, then followed them through the gap in the fence and into the old quarry. When they neared the rim of the rainwater-filled crater, one of the two men standing guard over Danny moved down the hill to meet them.

"Mrs. Vance, you've got yourself a scared, angry little boy up there," the man said, then glanced at Caleb. "Mr. Bishop, I'm not sure you should be here."

"I'm going up there to talk to him," Caleb said.

"I don't think that's a good idea. You're the one he's so upset with. He's liable to—"

"Mr. Bishop is going up there to talk to his son," Lowell Redman said. "He and Mrs. Vance have agreed on that."

"Thanks, Lowell," Caleb said, then turned and gave Sheila a hug.

He made his way up the steep, rocky embankment. When he reached the top, he saw Danny sitting near the edge on the opposite side. His heart tightened painfully at the sight of his son, dirty, tattered, obviously wet and cold.

Oh, God, please, let me say all the right things. Let me make him understand. Help me tell him exactly what he means to me.

"Danny!"

Danny snapped up his head and glared at Caleb. "Go away! I don't want to see you! I hate you!"

"I'm not going away, Danny."

"Why not? That's what you do, isn't it? You go away! You went away before I was born. And you'll go away again. But we don't care. Mom and I don't need you. We don't want you!"

"But I need you and your mom, Danny. I need you both and I want you more than I've ever wanted anything."

"Liar!" Danny stood abruptly. Rocks beneath his feet scattered and slid down the steep incline, splashing into the basin below. "You never wanted me. You don't want me now. All you ever wanted was to be a famous baseball player."

Please, God! Please! Don't let my son suffer because of my mistakes. Don't punish him. Punish me.

"Danny, I didn't know your mom was pregnant when I left town twelve years ago." Caleb sat, directly across from Danny.

"She didn't tell you because she knew you didn't want us!"

"I know why she didn't tell me." Caleb breathed deeply, taking air in and out in an effort to gain control of his own shattered emotions. "Your mom did what she thought was best for all three of us. You see, Danny, she loved me and she—"

"But you didn't love her! You didn't love me! And you don't love us now."

"Danny, that's..." He wouldn't lie to his son. There had been enough lies, no matter how well-intentioned, between them. "When I was eighteen, I didn't love anybody but myself. All that mattered to me was what I wanted. I didn't deserve a wonderful woman like your mother or a great kid like you. But I'm not the same selfish boy I was then. Danny, I'm a different kind of man now."

Danny stood near the edge—too close—his long, thin legs unsteady. He covered his ears with his hands. "I don't want to hear any more of your lies!"

"I'm not lying to you, Danny. I promise that I'm telling you the truth. No, I didn't love your mom twelve years ago and I don't know if I'd have given up my baseball scholarship if she'd told me she was pregnant. Probably not."

Danny eased his hands away from his ears, narrowed his gaze and glared at Caleb. "Now, you're telling me the truth."

"But that was then," Caleb said. "Things are different now. I'm different. Son, I—"

"Don't you call me son! Daniel Vance was my father! I'm no son of yours!"

"You're right, Danny. Daniel Vance was your father in all the ways that count. He loved you and took care of you and was there when you needed him. But the truth is that I'm your biological father and nothing can change that fact."

"I don't want to be…your son." Danny's voice broke with emotion.

"I love you, Danny," Caleb said. "I started loving you months ago, before I had any idea you were mine. And now… Can't you give me a second chance? I'll do anything if you'll forgive me and let me try to make it up to you."

Sheila climbed to the top of the cavern wall and made her way over to Caleb. When Danny noticed his mother, his gaze focused on her. Caleb glanced up at her and then back to Danny.

"Danny, please…" Sheila bit down on her bottom lip.

"You lied to me," Danny said. "You let me idolize him.

You let me think he was my best buddy. And all the while you knew he was my father and that he didn't want me. He never wanted me.''

"Yes, I lied to you," Sheila admitted. "I tried to protect you. Maybe what I did was wrong, but…" She swallowed hard. "I love you, Danny. You've been my whole life. I'm so sorry that you had to find out the truth the way you did. I had hoped Caleb and I could tell you together.''

"Do you believe him? Do you really think he's different now than he was then?" Danny asked.

"Yes, Danny, I do believe him. And I wish you would, too. Caleb does love you and he wants to be a father to you. He won't ever leave you again."

"What about you, Mom?" Danny looked directly at Caleb. "Does he love you, too?"

"I don't know," she replied. "Why don't you ask Caleb?"

"Do you?" Danny asked. "Do you love my mother? And don't lie to me. I'll know if you're lying."

Caleb looked at Sheila. Maybe there were women more beautiful. Women who were sexier. But not to him. To him, Sheila was the most perfect woman in the world. The only woman in the world for him. Just being with her made him happy. Did he love her? Yes. Of course, he loved her. Why had he ever thought loving someone was such a complicated emotion? Why had he questioned his own feelings when he'd known, deep down inside, that what he felt for Sheila was the real thing? He'd never cared for anyone the way he cared for her. It was that simple. Love was that simple.

I love you. He mouthed the words in a whisper and when she smiled, he knew she'd read his lips. He faced his son and said, "Yes, Danny, I love your mother. I love her very much and…and I had planned to ask her to marry me last night. I've got the ring right here." Caleb felt around inside his jacket pocket and pulled out the velvet box. "See." He flipped open the box and held it out toward Danny.

"You really were going to propose to her?" Danny stared at the ring, his big blue eyes filled with tears.

"More than anything I want your mother and you." Caleb glanced over at Sheila and then back to Danny. "If y'all will give me a second chance, I promise I'll never let either of you down again. I'll never leave you."

"I don't know." Danny took a hesitant step toward his parents, then stopped suddenly. "If you ever hurt my mom again, I'll—I'll make you sorry."

Sheila trembled from head to toe. She sucked in her cheeks, trying desperately to hold back the tears. Her little man. Such a protective son.

She opened her arms. "Come on, Danny. Please, sweetheart, let's go home. We'll find a way to work out all the problems."

"Okay. But I'm not making any promises."

As if viewing a nightmare and unable to prevent what was happening, they watched Danny start toward them, noticed how precariously close he was to the edge and saw the rocks beneath his feet slide, taking him with them in their downward plunge.

Sheila screamed. Caleb's heart stopped beating for a split second. Danny's body scraped against the rough, rock surface as it descended. His head bounced into a protruding boulder. He hit the water and disappeared beneath the surface.

"Oh, God!" Sheila hurried to the edge. "He could be unconscious. I have to get to him."

"Stay here." Caleb grasped her shoulders and shook her. "I'll get Danny."

Caleb climbed down the steep, rocky incline until he cleared the most hazardous area, then dove into the murky depths of the rain-filled cavern.

Sheila waited, her heart in her throat. This couldn't be

happening. Her son and his father both in danger. Everything that mattered to her was in jeopardy. With every breath she took, she prayed. *Give us all a second chance. Not for me or for Caleb. But for Danny's sake. He deserves to have a family.*

Caleb came to the surface. He rose empty-handed. Alone. *Where is Danny?* Sheila cried out silently.

Lowell Redman placed his hand on Sheila's shoulder. "The rescue squad's here. Their team is going around over there, where they can get to the edge of the water easier."

Caleb gulped in air, then dove again. Sheila ignored everything and everyone else around her. She concentrated on the surface of the dark pool. Overhead the sun broke through the morning clouds and light spread out across the earth like a golden, life-giving shower.

Caleb returned to the surface. Danny clung to his father as they came up out of the water. The rescue team reached them quickly, taking Danny first and then Caleb. Sheila dropped to her knees. Tears cascaded off her face and ran down her neck.

"They're both alive," one of the paramedics hollered.

Lowell lifted Sheila to her feet and kept his arm around her as he helped her down the side of the hill. She ran toward the stretcher on which Danny lay, reaching him just as the medics lifted him into the ambulance. She hurled herself into the back of the vehicle and leaned over her son.

Danny opened his eyes and looked up at her. "He saved my life, didn't he? I don't remember exactly what happened. I must have hit my head when I fell. All I remember is falling and the next thing I knew Caleb was bringing me up out of the water."

"Oh, Danny. I was so afraid I'd lost you." Sheila caressed her son's cheeks, then kissed him over and over again.

"Where's Caleb?" Danny asked.

Sheila looked out the open doors of the ambulance and

saw Caleb only a few feet away, his broad shoulders wrapped in a blanket. Their gazes met. She motioned for him to come to them.

"Here he is," she told Danny.

Danny tried to lift his head, but the medic eased him down gently. "You've probably got a concussion, young man. I want you to lie still until we get you checked out at the hospital."

"I don't want to go to the hospital."

"You're going." Sheila used her most authoritarian voice.

"But I want to see Caleb!"

"I'm right here, slugger." Caleb crawled into the back of the ambulance alongside Sheila.

"Tell 'em I don't have to go to the hospital," Danny whined. "I'm okay. Just some scrapes and bruises. Tell Mom that we're tough and going to the hospital is sissy stuff."

"We may be tough," Caleb said, his hand hesitantly lingering over Danny's head. "But even tough guys like us need to humor the women we love, don't we? It'll make your mom feel a lot better if you and I go to the hospital and let a doctor check us out."

"You're going, too?" Danny twisted his head around so he could get a better look at Caleb.

Caleb cupped the top of Danny's head. "I sure am. I can't have your mom worrying about me."

"Okay. I'll go, too." Danny looked up at his mother. "Hey, don't cry. We're both all right."

"I know. I'm crying because I'm so happy." Sheila buried her face against Caleb's chest.

He wrapped his arms around her, looked down at Danny and winked.

Danny winked back at him. Caleb turned away as tears filled his eyes. Dear God, he'd come so close to losing his son.

Sheila felt the teardrops as they fell against her cheek. They weren't her tears. She lifted her head and looked at Caleb. He was crying. The big, tough man she'd fallen in love with all these years ago, was actually crying.

"Okay, you two, smile." Danny aimed the camera at his parents, who turned around and bestowed beaming smiles on him. He snapped the picture. "Now, Mom, hold up your hand and let me get a shot of that big ring."

Sheila held up her left hand, where Caleb's ruby and diamond engagement ring shimmered on her third finger. "How many more pictures are you going to take? You've already used up a whole roll of film."

"You want your engagement party documented, don't you?" Danny focused the zoom lens on the camera and took a closeup of his mother's ring.

The country club buzzed with life as two-thirds of Crooked Oak's residents milled around the most celebrated party the town had ever seen. Caleb Bishop was getting married to hometown girl Sheila Hanley Vance. And despite a few ugly tidbits of gossip about Danny's true paternity, the town as a whole considered Sheila and Caleb's union a long overdue blessing.

With his arm around Sheila, Caleb leaned over and whispered, "I wish the wedding was tomorrow. I'm tired of spending nights alone at my house."

"You can wait another three weeks," Sheila told him. "We're setting a good example for our son. Remember?"

"He's starting to accept me, isn't he?" Caleb smiled, watching Danny as he made his way around the room taking snapshots of their guests.

"It'll take time, but eventually, he'll accept you completely. One day, you'll really be his father."

"That day won't come too soon for me," Caleb told her. "I lost the first eleven years of his life. I don't want to lose any more time with him."

"I think he knows that."

"Yeah, I think he does." Caleb led Sheila out onto the dance floor. "I was wondering what Danny would say if I asked him to be my best man at our wedding."

"Oh, Caleb. What a sweet idea. Why don't you ask him and see what he says?"

They danced their way across the room until they spotted Danny again. He was taking a picture of Lowell and Susan Redman.

"You got a minute, slugger?" Caleb asked.

"Yeah, sure. What is it?" Danny came over to his parents.

"You know the wedding is only three weeks off and...well, Susan is going to be your mom's matron of honor and... It's like this, Danny. I need a best man."

"You've got two brothers, don't you?"

"Yes, and Hank has promised to be here for the wedding, but I had hoped my son—that is, I'd hoped you might want to be my best man."

"Me? Are you kidding?"

"It would mean a great deal to me if you would."

"Gee, I don't know, Caleb. Can I think about it and let you know?"

"Sure you can."

Sheila slid her arm around Caleb's waist, leaned over and kissed him on the cheek. "Be patient with him. Give him some time."

"I'll give him all the time he needs."

Epilogue

Crooked Oak's Congregational Church was filled to capacity and the overflow stood outside the building, where loudspeakers had been set up so that the press could cover Caleb Bishop's wedding. *The wedding of the decade*. The former superstar playboy was marrying his former high school sweetheart, according to all the worldwide headlines.

Governor Peyton Rand and his first lady, Tallie Bishop Rand, had arrived surrounded by bodyguards, and a squad of private security officers mingled with the guests, inside and out. The crowd outside the church quieted when the processional music began. A woman standing just inside the doorway whispered loudly, "The bride's attendants' dresses are bronze and they're all carrying white daisies tied with bronze ribbon."

The women in the crowd oohed and ahhed. "Sheila's dress is candlelight cream and she's carrying a huge bouquet of daisies. She's absolutely beautiful."

Sheila held Mike's arm and waited while Tallie and Susan strolled down the left aisle and Hank and Lowell went down the right one. This day was a dream come true for her—a fairy-tale ending for a romance that had begun so long ago. Who but a true romantic would have believed a girl like her would wind up marrying Prince Charming? Today she felt very special. In fact, she felt beautiful. As beautiful as Caleb had told her she was. Perhaps love really was blind. She smiled.

The wedding march began. Mike led her down the flower-strewn aisle. Caleb waited for her at the altar—Caleb, the man she loved with all her heart. And beside him stood their son, a younger, shorter replica of his father. These days, no one who saw the two together could help but notice the striking resemblance.

Danny's agreeing to be Caleb's best man had given them hope for the future—hope that their little boy was willing to truly forgive them and help the three of them become a real family.

Caleb joined hands with his bride. He thanked God for the chance to do it right this time. Twelve years ago he hadn't been worthy of a woman like Sheila. He still might not deserve her, but now he was man enough to try to be the husband she wanted and the father Danny needed.

They exchanged vows, pledging their love and their lives. And in words they had written themselves, they made solemn promises to their son. By the time the minister said, "You may kiss your bride," there wasn't a dry eye in the house.

"I'd like to introduce Mr. and Mrs. Caleb Bishop," Reverend Swan said.

"And son," Caleb whispered to the minister.

"Yes, yes. Mr. and Mrs. Caleb Bishop and son."

As they faced the congregation, comprised of family, friends and supportive acquaintances, Caleb and Sheila reached over and pulled Danny between them. Together the threesome came down the aisle and walked outside, where the governor's private security officers made a path to the waiting limousine.

"You two go on," Danny said. "I'll ride with Uncle Hank and Lowell."

"We want you to ride with us, son," Caleb said.

"Okay, Dad, I'll ride with y'all to the reception, but I draw the line at going with you and Mom on your honeymoon."

At that moment Caleb thought his heart would burst with happiness. He had everything a man could want. He was the luckiest husband and father in the whole world.

"It's a deal," Caleb told his son. "If you don't go on our honeymoon, I promise your mother and I won't go on yours."

The three of them laughed as the driver headed the limousine toward the country club and the happy celebration of their love and lifelong commitment.

* * * * *

*Don't miss
Hank Bishop's story,
HIS WOMAN, HIS CHILD
coming in April 1999 as
Beverly Barton's emotional miniseries,
3 BABIES FOR 3 BROTHERS, continues.
Only from Silhouette Desire!*

Beloved author
BEVERLY BARTON
brings an exciting new miniseries to Desire!

March 1999: HIS SECRET CHILD (SD#1203)
One sultry night, Sheila Vance lost herself in Caleb Bishop's
arms. And unknown to him, Caleb became a father. Now the
seductive bachelor was back and he had Sheila trembling…

April 1999: HIS WOMAN, HIS CHILD (SD#1209)
He was the man she'd always loved, and now fate had made
Hank Bishop the father of Susan Redman's unborn child.
Susan dreamed of forever with the sexy loner who'd vowed
never to fall in love.…

May 1999: HAVING HIS BABY (SD#1216)
When Donna Fields returned from her trip out West, she brought
home more than just memories. Nine months later, Jake Bishop
was back in town and out to convince sweet Donna that even a
brooding loner could be a devoted dad—and a loving husband.

3 Babies for 3 Brothers: *There's nothing like a secret baby
to bring a brooding bachelor home again!*

Only from 🔶 *Silhouette*®

Available at your favorite retail outlet.

If you enjoyed what you just read,
then we've got an offer you can't resist!

Take 2 bestselling love stories FREE!

Plus get a FREE surprise gift!

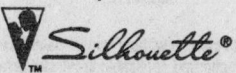